I couldn't enjoy the aroma as I normally ~~did~~
Cherry blossoms, smelling like spring.

It had meant death for Charla. Some darkish specks stood out against the pink soap-scrub flakes. What was this? The small nubbins didn't belong in this scrub.

Once I found a clean bowl, I heaped a few generous scoops of scrub into it and pushed the flakes around with my finger. I lifted a palmful to my nose and inhaled.

Cherry. . .and something else. The wild tang also bore a hint of different sweetness. Of strawberries?

Don't miss out on a single one of our great mysteries. Contact us at the following address for information on our newest releases and club information:

Heartsong Presents—MYSTERIES! Readers' Service
PO Box 721
Uhrichsville, OH 44683
Web site: www.heartsongmysteries.com

Or for faster action, call 1-740-922-7280.

A Suspicion of Strawberries

A Scents of Murder Mystery

Lynette Sowell

HEARTSONG
PRESENTS
MYSTERIES

Many, many thanks to my critique partners—Susan Page Davis, Darlene Franklin, and Lisa Harris. Your input and encouragement mean so much. I'm glad we all found each other.

Christine Lynxwiler, thanks for being a friend and for cheering me on when I first started this project. Rachel Hauck and Brandilyn Collins, thank you for sharing your knowledge of the craft and for answering my questions. I love how you set the bar high, and I aim to keep learning from both of you. Candice Speare and Ellen Tarver, you can be on my editing team any day.

Of course, I dedicate this with much love to my dear husband and kids. Thank you for your patience with me, for never allowing me to quit, and for seeing what I often don't see. And here's to my out-laws and in-laws in Tennessee. Love y'all!

© 2008 by Lynette Sowell

ISBN 978-1-59789-523-1

All scripture quotations are taken from the King James Version of the Bible.

This book is a work of fiction. Names, characters, places, and incidents are either products of the author's imagination or used fictitiously. Any similarity to actual people, organizations, and/or events is purely coincidental.

Cover Design: Kirk DouPonce, DogEared Design
Cover Illustration: Jody Williams

Our mission is to publish and distribute inspirational products offering exceptional value and biblical encouragement to the masses.

Printed in the United States of America.

Mornings can be murder, especially when they start with a broken coffeepot. I glanced at my wrist as I sped down Main Street in my Jeep. Of course, I'd forgotten my watch. That didn't keep me from stopping at the Higher Grounds pickup window to grab a venti double-shot caramel café mocha. No matter that it was early June and the hot coffee would make me melt. This Saturday morning, my body definitely needed the caffeine jolt before bride-to-be Charla Thacker and her gaggle of bridesmaids descended on Tennessee River Soaps.

The upcoming wedding a week from today had to be the biggest summer event in Greenburg, Tennessee, population 9,973. I'm sure most of the business owners involved could recite the details. As for my little part in the prewedding festivities, Charla had taken forever to decide on Cherries Jubilee facial scrub for her and her bridesmaids. In that space of time, I had learned about the five-figure price tag of her diamond, the house everyone already knew about on the riverfront, and the planned honeymoon to the Grand Caymans. I even had to look that one up on the map. Most of the time the locals enjoyed vacations to Florida or perhaps California or a cruise, but of course Charla had to be different. Which leads me to her plans for a "spa day" for her bridesmaids.

Now Greenburg isn't exactly the sticks, but it

doesn't really have anything resembling a spa. So after a bit of exfoliation at my store that morning, the young women planned to pile back into someone's car and head to the next stop—probably The Gazebo—for massages and pedicures. Then, the grand finale at the Venetian Tea Room down the road—a special "cleansing" lunch. A sampling of Greenburg's best little businesses. Instead of a progressive dinner, Charla was treating her best friends to a progressive total spa package. I'm surprised she didn't take out an ad in the paper announcing each phase of the journey.

Charla's flair for the dramatic included stunts like cruising down Main Street one Saturday night with her upper torso stuck through the top of her friend's sunroof, waving her arms and hollering at anyone who'd notice. And that was just the night she and Robert Robertson got engaged. We all thought she'd won the lottery or something. Not that she needed the money.

I flashed by a string of small storefronts and pulled up in front of a neat little cottage shop, white with Wedgwood blue trim. *Mine.* Well, mine for the modest rent payment I dropped off at the leasing company every month. My fingers still burned from signing the paperwork. Six months later, the business floated like Ivory soap, but barely. The place is my baby, a combination of in-store soap sales and Internet orders. Hey, if the rest of the world can sell on the Web, so can I—right here in Greenburg. I drove around to the side of the building where I usually parked.

Then I saw the side door. Splintered wood surrounded a jimmied lock, the door ajar. I hit the brakes so hard my coffee sloshed through the opening in its lid. The cup tipped over the edge of the cup holder and poured onto the passenger side floor mat.

Not a break-in. *Please, Lord, not at Tennessee River Soaps. Not to me.* Greenburg in the summer means kids out of school with little to do. Without many job prospects, what can you expect? Jerry at the Greenburg PD had his hands full. Now I'd have to call him to come down, my business another statistic like other businesses in town that summer.

I found my cell phone at the bottom of my hobo bag, among the old receipts and empty gum wrappers, and called the station. "This is Andi—er, Andromeda Clark at Tennessee River Soaps on Main Street. I'd like to report a break-in." As expected, I spelled my name, just as I had countless other times in my life. *Thanks, Dad.* An armchair space buff, he made up for never becoming an astronaut by naming me after a constellation.

Once I finished the call with the dispatcher, assuring her it wasn't an emergency but to hurry, I waited in the Jeep. After twenty minutes of listening to the radio and watching the pine trees sway in the June breeze, I debated going inside the store anyway. The humidity promised a hot day. Still no Jerry or one of his men. Maybe if I used the end of my shirt, or bumped the door open with my hip, I could get inside the building without messing up any incriminating fingerprints. But the dispatcher had told me to wait outside until an officer arrived.

Visions of a demolished store taunted my mind. I wanted to burst through the door of the shop, grab some disinfectant spray, and start cleaning. Another thought grabbed me. Should I call Charla Thacker and cancel her appointment? *I can't believe this happened.*

Jerry arrived before I dialed the station again. He left the squad car and ambled over to the side door. Hartley men don't hurry. I should know this. His brother, Ben, my boyfriend, only rushes on the first weekend of hunting season. Today Ben was probably somewhere in his tractor-trailer rig between Jackson and Cleveland. The two brothers rattled around in a big house that used to belong to their parents. I longed to play matchmaker for Jerry, but I couldn't bear to think of the disaster after my last attempt.

Of course, all of Greenburg probably wondered when Ben and I would eventually tie the knot. I didn't know which made me antsier: the thought of a wedding or the unknown that waited for me inside the store.

Jerry shook his head and perspiration dripped from his forehead and sandy hair. It just wasn't legal for a man to have hair that nice. Ben did, too, but shaved his curly locks close in a buzz. "Looks like your place was next in the series of break-ins this summer. Number three this month."

I left the Jeep and joined him at the door. "I didn't touch anything or go in yet."

"We'll have a look around." Jerry slipped his gun

from his holster, nudged the door with his shoulder, and went into the workroom. After a few seconds, he emerged, sticking the gun back in its place. "Can't be too careful. Looks clear."

Good old Jerry, telling me what I already knew. Of course they had to be long gone. It wasn't like I had anything worth stealing. "Listen, Jer." I craned my neck to look around him. "Charla Thacker's bridal party invades in about an hour, and I haven't had my coffee."

"All right, go on in." I pushed past him and into the back room where I prepared my concoctions. The surface of the stainless steel worktable gleamed, just like I'd left it last night. I expelled a pent-up sigh when I saw the undisturbed bowls of cherry facial scrub I'd mixed especially for Charla's party, and the big, covered vat of cherry scrub I'd planned to package for sale afterward. All of the other products looked untouched, as well.

Jerry entered the room behind me. "You were one of the fortunate victims. Millie over at Rags Fifth Avenue had to get new carpet installed after the thieves got through with her store. Good thing no one vandalized your shop and dumped those pretty little soaps all over the place." *Pretty little soaps.* I tried not to grimace. In happier circumstances, the phrase would have made me smile. Most guys didn't get it. Give 'em a bar of soap from The Dollar Shoppe and they're happy.

The spring and summer stock looked fine, from Peachy Keen to June Breeze to Cherries Jubilee, their packaging intact. Thankful for that, I entered the salesroom. The cash register was open, its drawer a yawning chasm of plastic. Evidently these guys knew what they wanted when they came in.

"They got my starting cash, fifty dollars." I pointed at the empty drawer, and Jerry jotted something down. "But it doesn't look like anything else is missing." After I glanced around at the soap displays, I looked at the clock. No time to clean anything, but I didn't like the idea that someone had been in *my* store without *my* permission.

Jerry touched my arm. "I'm sorry this happened. From what Ben said, sales were picking up for you."

"Yes, I've been doing pretty well." And with today's good publicity, thanks to Charla and her friends, hopefully business would pick up a lot. "And I'm sure you'll catch whoever did this."

Jerry scanned my workroom. "I'll get Margaret to come down here with her print kit and dust. See what we can find."

That's all I needed. Sure, I wanted to get whoever did this, but I didn't want cops underfoot while Charla and her group were here. What if Charla turned up her nose and walked out at the disruption?

"Could she wait, until maybe noonish? I promise I won't touch the register. I'll even cover it with a bag if you want."

Jerry grunted. "I guess. . ."

"Everything I need is already out on sales-floor tables, and no one else has to go in the back room."

He nodded and chucked me on the arm. "We'll do our best to find out who did this." Then he clapped his notepad shut on his hip. "If we get any leads, I'll let you know. Oh. Ben called late last night. He should be arriving in time for church tomorrow."

I smiled at that, and my heart sang. "That's the best news I've heard all morning."

"See you around." With that, Jerry nodded and left the store the way he came in.

But what I wished for was Ben here right *now*. The man was as immovable as the Rock of Gibraltar. He had a way of staying cool under pressure. I envied that. When my stress level escalated, I felt like Momma's old pressure cooker, ready to burst.

I left the empty cash drawer alone and saw to making coffee. Of course, I'd lost my gourmet cup of coffee to the Jeep's floor. All I could do was dash out the back door and cover the mess in the Jeep with generous layers of paper towels. Already I felt the twinges of a caffeine headache at my temples.

Once the two-cup coffeepot gurgled from its spot on my desk in the office nook, I went back to the Cherries Jubilee scrub on my worktable in the back room. The small bowls of scrub, no larger than cereal bowls, didn't look full enough. Not wanting to have Charla accuse me of being stingy with the product, I dumped another scoopful of the flakes from the large storage vat into each bowl. Then I replaced the clear plastic lids and shook the covered bowls.

The demonstration table waited in the main sales-room. At each guest's place there was a small make-up mirror, a cherry red placemat, and a few samples of other products along with my business card and coupons. I smiled for the first time since discovering the break-in. Momma would say I needed to thank God I'd only lost fifty dollars, and so I did. Last thing, I grabbed a pitcher, filled it with water, and set it on the table.

Only thirty minutes to—

———

"Showtime!" Charla Thacker breezed into the shop. A rush of laughter followed her. Even the bell on the door clanged with joy. Twenty-five and at the height of her young femininity, the room seemed brighter when Charla entered. Maybe it was the summer sun shining at her back that ignited her blond hair's strawberry highlights. But she couldn't have planned that effect. Could she?

At ten years her senior, I caught a glimpse of what my mother once said about youth being wasted on the young. Charla's sister, Melinda, trailed closely behind, beautiful in her own right but possessing a more ethereal beauty like Romeo's Juliet instead of someone off the red carpet at the Oscars. Melinda's fair skin needed no exfoliating, and her hair glowed a rich shade of walnut in the sunlight. The other bridesmaids flowed into the room—Emily, Tess, and Mitchalene, I soon found out.

With my best "I'm-a-homespun-business-owner" smile on my face, I smoothed an imaginary wrinkle from my freshly starched Tennessee River Soaps apron.

"Good morning! I'm so glad you're here." I gestured to the round table in the center of the shop.

"Can we sit anywhere?" asked Melinda.

"*This* seat," I touched a chair festooned with cherry red crepe paper flowers, "is for the bride, of course. But y'all may sit anywhere else."

Charla waited by the chair, stared at it, then back to me. Oh, please, she wasn't waiting for me to pull the chair out for her.

I gritted my teeth and smiled, hoping I didn't look too much like a piranha. "Here you are." I slid the chair away from the table. Melinda rolled her eyes. Emily giggled. The movie screen in my brain projected a flashback to seventh grade in the lunchroom, when the queen bee of the grade made us tremble to do her bidding, except me. I'd ended up at a table by myself and more than once my carton of milk had gotten poured over my tray of food. Sometimes picking your battles wasn't easy. Greenburg had a social hierarchy that I both loathed and feared. How much to play along and be accepted? My cheeks hurt from smiling.

Charla settled herself onto the seat as if she were preparing to answer interview questions at a pageant. "Thank you. Now, Andromeda—"

I gritted my teeth again.

"Tell us about this product of yours." Charla pointed at the bowls.

"Cherries Jubilee is a new product I've come up with, and y'all are the first ones to sample it today. I've developed scented bath salts, hand soaps, and glycerin soaps, but now I've combined hot-processed soap with a moisturizer and sugar base into these dry flakes to make a scrub." I removed the lid from my own bowl and let the flakes run through my fingers. "What's nice about this is, you just add water, and you have a wonderfully gentle exfoliant. Plus, it smells like cherry pie, thanks to the essential oils added in the soap-making process." I grinned.

"Ooh, I can't wait." Charla rubbed her hands together. "This is so luxurious. I tried it once before, when Andromeda was making her first batch. She let me be her guinea pig."

My teeth were getting sore. "Right. She sure was." And she'd taken her sweet time making up her mind what scent she wanted. Strawberries were out. Allergic, she said, and she didn't want to risk a breakout before the wedding. Peach was too "nasty," she claimed. I wouldn't repeat what she said about cucumber melon.

Melinda snorted. "C'mon, Charla, you're getting on Ms. Clark's nerves." She made me sound like crotchety old Doris Flanders who used to chase kids from her watermelon patch with her shotgun.

"Don't worry about it." My face had frozen. I just knew it. "I'll demonstrate for you."

I poured a bit of water into my own bowl and continued. "You'll need to add a few tablespoons of water to the flakes and make a paste. Then take your wooden spatula like this, and stir well. You don't use your fingers, because the moisturizer starts acting immediately, and we want that process to happen on your face."

I can't believe I'm doing this. I, who was a flop at selling Vonna Cosmetics, demonstrating a beauty product to the elite of Greenburg. Who'd have thunk it? I started spreading the scrub on my face with the spatula and finally moved the scrub in a circular motion on my cheeks. At least I had good skin from skipping the tanning beds.

The young women removed the plastic covers from their bowls and mimicked my actions. Emily and Melinda had me check their mixes to make sure they'd added the correct amount of water to their flakes.

Charla dipped her wooden spatula into the scrub and swirled the mixture with vigor. "This smells heavenly." She smiled with her whitened teeth at her bridesmaids and swiped the first generous blob of scrub onto her cheeks. Then she grinned at herself in the small mirror propped up in front of her. She dolloped more scrub on her face.

The women chatted and giggled for a few minutes, and I encouraged them to gently rub the mixture in a circular motion on their skin while the moisturizer worked. Someone took a picture of Charla, her face all goopy.

"Ladies, I'll be right back." I smiled at the quintet whose main focus was themselves. "I'll get some damp rags so you can wipe the scrub from your faces in a few minutes." Melinda and Tess nodded.

I moved to the small sink in the corner where customers could try soap for themselves and ran a few washcloths under the water. When I returned, I noticed Charla rubbing her neck.

"Remember, your neck skin is a bit sensitive." I put a fresh smile on.

Charla coughed, then cleared her throat.

She frowned, and the room seemed to darken. "Oh." She slathered gobs of the scrub on her cheeks and forehead. "This doesn't feel right—"

What happened next moved in slow motion, like the time Ben and I went to the drive-in and saw *The Lion, the Witch, and the Wardrobe*, and the film got stuck and dragged, frame by frame.

I viewed each detail around the table as if posed and captured by the photographer in my head.

Charla, knocking the bowl away from her.

Cherry scrub splattering across the table.

Charla, grabbing her face, scratching at swelling cheeks.

Oblivious laughter from Emily and Tess.

Mitchalene scrubbing her own face for all she was worth.

Then everything shot into fast-forward mode.

Melinda leaped to her feet. "Charla!" She fell to her knees and scrambled on the floor for Charla's purse. "She's having an allergic reaction!" All laughter stopped.

"What?" I grabbed a damp cloth and soaked it in the pitcher of water, then started wiping scrub from Charla's face. I could barely see her eyes for the swelling. *Jesus, help us!*

Melinda dumped the contents of Charla's purse

onto the table. "Where's her EpiPen? It's not here. She's always leaving it at home. Oh, c'mon, Charla, how could you?" The other girls stared with mouths agape.

"Someone call 911—"

I ran for the phone and dialed. "Please, we need an ambulance at 564 Main. A woman's having a severe allergic reaction—hurry!" I threw the phone down, leaving the dispatcher on the line. He called to me from the phone, but I ran back to Melinda.

She and Emily had dragged Charla to the floor, where her breaths came in ragged gasps. "Hang on! Hang on! Help's coming!" Melinda's wide-eyed gaze darted around the room. "Benadryl? Anyone have Benadryl?" No one did.

I knelt down next to Charla and prayed in whispers, holding her hand that now squeezed mine in a viselike grip. Her body shook in spasms.

"What's taking so long?" Melinda wailed.

I ran back to the phone and grabbed the receiver. "Where's the ambulance? She can't breathe. We don't have Benadryl or an EpiPen."

"Ma'am, they're en route. They've just left County Hospital and are about five minutes out. Try to keep her airway clear."

"Okay, okay, we'll try." I flew back to Charla's side. "She said they'll be here in about five minutes."

Charla's eyelids fluttered, then closed. "No–o!" Melinda wailed.

"Tilt her head back." My basic first-aid training took over. "Try to keep her airway open." I felt her pulse, racing too quickly for me to count. *Lord, no, please!*

"Her pen's got to be here!" Melinda went back to the table, where the other girls stood, clasping hands to mouths. Mitchalene's face was streaked with tears.

Charla's fingers were turning blue, her lips now a deep purple and twice their normal size. Not good. A siren wailed in the distance. Tess ran for the door.

Melinda sank to her knees beside her sister. "Charla. . .no, no, no. . ." She brushed silken blond strands back from Charla's forehead, now distorted and mottled with red welts.

Charla's body gave one last great convulsion, her arms flailing like a rag doll's. I closed my eyes. The siren's wail intensified. The pulse under my fingertips grew still.

2

The ambulance left without using its sirens. I watched it glide away down Main Street. Clusters of people gathered on the sidewalk. A few onlookers squinted from the parking lot of the Antiques Barn across the street, so I reentered my store. Not long now, and news would spread. Melinda sat in Charla's chair, its red paper flowers crushed. Emily sat next to her, crying. Tess and Mitchalene were busy on their cell phones, presumably trying to secure rides home. I wanted to throw up. I'd skipped breakfast that morning, and the only food I brought with me was a ziplock bag of my sister Diana's homemade beef jerky.

As much as Charla had grated on my nerves, I never would have wished anything like this to happen to her, or to anyone. Jerry, for the second time that morning, came to the shop. A rookie officer questioned the bridesmaids, then left. Maggie dusted the register for fingerprints. Like that mattered now. A heavy stillness hung in the store. At last I realized I still had Cherries Jubilee scrub drying on my face, so I grabbed a washcloth to wipe it off.

Jerry jotted something on his notepad and approached me. "What were y'all doing again?"

"Facial scrub. . ." With my free hand, I picked up the bowl Charla had used. "She was fine until. . ." I closed my eyes.

"Until she put that stuff on her face." Melinda finished for me. Her glare would have made me flinch if I wasn't so numb.

"I don't understand. I *made* this scrub before and Charla used it. Charla told me she was allergic to certain ingredients, and I made sure the scrub contained none of those."

Emily sat up straighter in her chair. "Charla liked to push it, though. Last week she snuck a bite of my strawberry pie over at Honey's Place." I nodded in understanding. Honey's had the best food in town, and their homemade pies were to die for. Maybe not literally to die for, but. . . I frowned.

Melinda shot Emily a look. "And that stunt you pulled on Valentine's Day wasn't even funny. You should be glad she had her EpiPen after eating a chocolate bon bon filled with strawberry nougat."

A flush swept over Emily's face. She glanced from me, to Jerry, then back at Melinda. "She wore my new sweater to that party without asking me. I know, I was being stupid and immature, now that I think about it." Fresh tears came from Emily's eyes. "But that's just it, I didn't think. . . . Oh, Charla. . .if I could take it back."

"You've got nothing to worry about. This is just an unfortunate incident." Jerry turned from them and gestured to me. "I have to submit a sample of that soap to the lab for testing." He almost sounded apologetic, and I couldn't blame him.

"Do what you need to do." I pushed the container

into Jerry's hands. Now wasn't the time to ask questions, especially with Melinda here.

"Miss Thacker, I'm really sorry." Jerry glanced at her. "Do you need someone to come get you?"

Melinda shook her head. "Emily'll drive me to Mom and Dad's." A tear rolled down her cheek, now free of scrub. After the initial uproar had quieted, I had passed around the wet washcloths to both soothe the women and let them clean their faces.

Tess moved to give Melinda a hug. "Hey, my sister just pulled up. She's takin' me and Mitch home. I'll call ya later." Melinda nodded. Without a word to me or a look in my direction, Tess and Mitchalene left the store.

I sat down at the round table. "Melinda—"

"Don't talk to me right now." The words stabbed at me. "Em, get me out of here." They snatched up their purses and left the store.

Jerry was leaning against a glycerin-soap display. "I need to file my report. You gonna be all right?"

I nodded. "I'm going to call Ben."

"That's a fine idea." With that, he left me alone with the memory of the tragedy fresh in my mind. I sat down and did the next logical thing. I prayed. I didn't know why this tragedy had happened, but I prayed for Charla's family. What Melinda must be going through, her parents, and Robert, Charla's fiancé. The thought of how they must feel made me want to cry. My sister, Diana, once told me I have the gift of empathy, if that's a gift. Sometimes I don't like the sensation of wearing someone else's shoes.

I shifted to safer territory and prayed that God would show me what to do next, that He would protect my business somehow—and my reputation. The petition made me feel shallow. But I'd worked so hard on Tennessee River Soaps. For once, I wanted to succeed in Greenburg.

As I walked around the shop, I prayed, touching the bins of scoop-and-bag-it-yourself bath salts. I picked up one of the molded glycerin soaps. A pale blue background surrounded a taupe swirl that looked like a seashell. *Maybe this is frivolous, Lord, but for once in my life, I believe I'm doing something right.*

My cell phone warbled before I got to *amen. Ben!*

I punched the button. "Hey, hon, I'm sure glad it's you."

"Jerry left a message, said I needed to call you immediately." Already his baritone voice warmed me to my toes. "I just stopped for lunch. What's goin' on?"

Once I explained what had happened, his response was stillness on the other end of the line. Ben borders on being the silent type, but even for him this was unnerving.

"Ben?"

"That's horrible. How's her family?"

"Her sister's taking it hard. Which is understandable." My throat felt like I'd swallowed the sharp end of a potato chip. "Everything happened so fast."

"If it's any consolation, I don't think it was just that one scrub that killed her. I've heard some allergens build up in someone's system over time, and one little thing could send them into shock." Ben knew a little something about everything, his brain a virtual sponge.

"Where did you hear that?"

"I listen to a lot of talk radio on the road."

I wished I could reach through the phone and hug him. "I can't wait till you get home."

"Well, I'm on my way back now. I should be in Jackson by ten, and hopefully in Greenburg by midnight."

"I'll wait up if you want to call. I. . .I don't know how well I'll be able to sleep tonight." I despised the quaver in my voice. But sometimes I needed a bit of rescuing, no matter how hard I tried to run things.

"You want me to pray with you?"

"Sure." I listened to Ben's words pass over me like a breeze, then waft their way to heaven. He was a definite keeper. Charla could have her polished young lawyer who went for manicures and moisturizers, but I'd hang on to my gentle giant with a buzz cut who's a smidge rough around the edges. Except Charla didn't have her young lawyer anymore. *Oh, Lord, help her loved ones. And my attitude.*

"I'll call you tonight, Ands."

"I'll be waiting." But I wasn't done talking just yet. "You know what really bugs me?"

"What?" I heard the weariness in his voice. He was probably thinking, *Here goes Ands into one of her ramblings.* Okay, so I liked to think out loud.

"I *know* that scrub had nothing in it that Charla

would have been allergic to. I mixed it myself, using the exact recipe Charla and I played with a month ago. She mentioned that she'd had reactions to strawberries, peanuts, and mangos. But this was *cherry* scrub." I smacked my countertop for emphasis.

"Baby, there's just some things we can't explain."

"Well, I know the scrub was fine. I refuse to believe otherwise." I moved back to the table in the center of the shop. The bowls still lay where the young women had set them down. One had ended up on the floor somehow. Cherry scrub was already starting to dry onto the laminate surface of the table.

"Sometimes things happen. You didn't do anything wrong. Did Jerry happen to take any of that goop for the lab?"

"Yeah, he did. It'll take forever to hear back, though."

"I'm sure he'll give you a copy of the report."

"I just don't like waiting." I tried not to sigh.

"Neither do I." His affection oozed through the line. "I can't wait to see you."

"I miss you, too." My throat tightened. "Well, I'd better get off the phone so you can get back on the road."

"I love you, Ands."

"I love you, too." The phone clicked, and I closed the cover.

Ben, Ben, Ben, Ben, Ben. What was I going to do? I missed his voice when he was away, the strength of his arms, the dimple in his right cheek when he was embarrassed. His little-boy joy at discovering something new. The man was a fact magnet. Yet when he was in town for too long, *I* sometimes felt like I wanted to run and hit the road. But it wasn't him. It was me.

If I dropped a few hints, I'd probably have a diamond bright enough to blind someone. Not as over-the-top as Charla's ring, but it would be mine. Ben worked hard and was frugal with his money but lavish with his love.

So I came back around to the inevitable question. *What is wrong with me?*

I already knew I couldn't imagine being without him. Trouble was, I didn't know how I could be with him. Every day. All the time. Day in and day out.

The bell over the front door clanged. I tried not to cringe before I looked up. I'd forgotten to lock the door. Then I smiled at Diana, my sister with the more normal name. Momma had put her foot down when Diana was born.

"I came as soon as I could get away from the drive-through window." She flicked her hair over her shoulder and plopped onto the chair next to me, her brown eyes round, her eyebrows raised. "What in the world happened?"

"I don't know what you heard, but the rumor around town is probably that my facial scrub killed Charla Thacker."

Diana touched my arm. At the bank, her hands touched more money than we'd ever have in our lifetime. "All I heard was an accident happened at your shop and something about Charla. But I've been frantic wantin' to find out. Did you talk to Ben?"

"I just did. He'll be home tonight."

"Oh, that's good." Diana, an old soul, had a soothing way about her much like Momma's. "What about you? Are you all right?"

I nodded. "But I need to pick your brain." I reached for one of the bowls that still hadn't made it to the storage room. "Something in this scrub killed her, but I haven't a clue what it was or how it got into the containers."

Diana opened the bowl and sniffed. "Did she try to eat it?"

"Of course not." I shook my head. "She put it on her face and—*bam!*"

"It's not your fault." Her calming tone didn't have the same effect on me that it usually did.

"I know it's not, but you know how people talk. Small towns have the longest memories." I spread my arms out as if to embrace the room. "I'm heartsick over what happened to Charla, but I put so much into this business."

"More than even the rug-weaving business you started, or the pottery shop, or the gourmet cookie business?"

My face flamed. "Those flopped. This place has a chance. Or had." God made me creative. I'd had a hard time focusing that gift until I opened Tennessee River Soaps.

Diana pointed at me. "Those businesses didn't flop. They struggled. I might not have finished my business degree, but I know that businesses have growing pains, face struggles, and have setbacks. You have so much talent and creativity. You can't quit because of what happened to Charla. No matter what people say."

It was my turn to point at her, but I instead pointed at the floor where Charla had lain until EMS had strapped her onto a gurney and rolled her from the store. "She died right there. I don't know if I'd want to shop here either. The poor girl." I hadn't even thought about when to reopen for business. What sounded like a respectable amount of time, and what sounded uncaring? Still too early to tell.

"You know what you need to do?"

I shrugged.

"You need to close up shop, put this scrub on your worktable, and go home and turn off the phone. You've had a horrible shock. I know your first thoughts were for Charla's sister and friends, but you've been through an ordeal, too. I'll tell Momma and Daddy." Diana sounded so convincing. "She'll send some soup over for you or something."

"But my back door—the lock's been jimmied. Someone broke into the store last night."

"Huh? You didn't tell me that. When?" Her outrage normally would have amused me, but now I felt droopy with the adrenaline rush wearing off.

"Last night. What happened to Charla sort of overshadowed the break-in for a while." I explained what I'd found that morning.

Diana snapped her fingers. "I'll ask Steve to rig

something up for the door. In fact, I'll call him right now." Not only did she marry before I did, but she married a handyman. She found her cell phone, flipped it open, and dialed away.

Great. The matter of the break-in fought for attention again. I'd have to call the real estate company and tell them what happened. It wouldn't surprise me if my rent increased once the lease came up for renewal in a few more months. All over a broken door lock.

"Thanks, Di," was all I could manage to say while my thoughts overwhelmed me. I vacillated from shock over the break-in, what happened to Charla, and then to a flooding sense of empathy for Melinda, as if I'd been the one to lose a sister. A constricting feeling came into my throat. I struggled to catch my breath as a sense of overwhelming loss swept through me. *Lord, if anything like that ever happened to Di—*

"Peace."

I wrestled with my emotions while Diana chatted.

She snapped her phone shut and waved me off. "Now go. I'll wait for Steve here, and he'll put in a new lock." Diana sounded like she was addressing Taylor, my six-year-old nephew. "Stop worrying and borrowing trouble. 'Sufficient to the day is the evil thereof' and all that."

I stood and gave her half a smile then took off my canvas apron. I had to agree. So far today had contained enough trouble for a good long time.

3

Since I knew I'd be too busy working at the store to take any kind of vacation that summer, I had agreed to take the high school Sunday school class until September. I had thought about calling the Sunday school coordinator at church to see if she could find someone to take my class that morning, but I stopped myself. A substitute for the substitute. *Ha.* My Sunday routine would hold back the memories of Charla's body on the floor. The kids would make me laugh as they usually did.

As I surveyed the room filled with nine girls and five boys, I didn't regret the decision. This morning, however, stories flew around with a life of their own. I did my best, though, to deflect rumors with the truth. No one gave me accusing looks when I explained that Charla had tried the scrub before the party and it hadn't bothered her.

So I let them talk about what happened. . .to a point. The adult classes had coffee and doughnut time, better known as *fellowship*, so I figured the kids needed a chance to talk also. My stomach turned over on itself when I heard snatches of conversation.

"Her face was big as a balloon." One kid held his hands up around his face and puffed out his cheeks like a blowfish. "My brother's friend worked the ambulance yesterday."

"I heard a news story once about something like that happening to a girl after kissing her boyfriend." A brunette shook her long, curtainlike hair. "She was allergic to peanuts, and he'd had a peanut butter sandwich for lunch, hours and hours before."

"That's just so gross, you know. Didn't he brush his teeth?" another girl interjected. Oh, the practicality of teenagers.

"Where's Seth?" I scanned the faces in the room for the slim, dark-haired boy who had sat in the back last week. He hadn't participated, but I felt his challenging stare throughout the entire class.

Sadie, the girl who talked about the peanut butter kiss, spoke up. "He probably won't be here. He's Charla's cousin."

I nodded. "I see. Well, this seems like a good time to share prayer requests. We should pray for the Thacker family. Does anyone want to write down the requests so we can keep track?"

From the Thacker family to summer job needs to sick relatives and sunburns and someone wanting to get a car, we gathered the requests and prayed together. Sadie frowned. Her face looked as if her mind had just hit overdrive.

"Sadie, did you have a question?"

She blushed and looked around the room. "It probably doesn't have anything to do with the class, but I was wonderin' something about Charla. . . ."

Here we go. . .

"That's okay. Ask."

"I heard someone saying last night that it was about time Charla got a taste of her own medicine." Sadie's face went to a deeper shade of crimson. "I mean, who are they to say she got what she deserved?"

And I thought taking the high school group would be easy. I tried to find words that wouldn't sound trite to these kids. They could see through platitudes a mile away.

I swallowed hard before answering. "I look at it this way. God made Charla and had a plan for her life, like He does for everyone. I'm not Charla's judge, and I really didn't know her personally, but I don't think anyone deserves that kind of death. In the end, only God truly knows someone's heart. . . ." *Lord, help me; I'm sounding pretty lame. And I'm rambling. Ben would be in the back of the room, wondering when I'd stop trying to talk myself out of the hole I'm digging for myself.*

The dark-haired boy who talked about Charla's swollen face—Russ, if I read the roster correctly—sat up straighter in his chair. "So do you think God wanted her to die like that? I mean, we talked last week about Psalm 139 and how God knows all our days from beginning to end."

"Wow, y'all don't ask the easy questions, huh?" I clutched the podium a bit more tightly. *Next week we're going to move the chairs in a circle, and I'm going to sit down and not be on display.* "I'm not saying that God made that reaction happen to Charla. But the reality is we live in a fallen world. Bad things happen—to good people, bad people, and those people in between.

Sometimes it stinks. That's the reality of free will. But God still cares and sees. If He can see the sparrow fall and care about it, He cares no less for us. I don't know why this happened. I wish it hadn't. It's in times like this we really need to pour out to Him how we feel."

Again I felt the defensiveness from yesterday rising within me. *It's not my fault!* I looked down at my class notes. We were way off track, and we couldn't answer the tough questions of life in a forty-five-minute class.

"Well, maybe someone messed with your soap."

The statement hung in the air like a trumpet's call, and I glanced around the room to see who'd spoken. Sadie, the Thinker.

"What?" I understood her perfectly, but I didn't quite believe she'd said it.

"Really, Miss Clark. If you know you did everything right with that face scrub and it didn't bother her when she tried it before, the simplest explanation is that somebody else messed with your soap."

The break-in. Was it more than mere coincidence? My mind whirled. But who? How? Most important, why? I promptly dismissed her conclusion as the fervent wish of youth to see justice served, to find an explanation for the inexplicable.

I smiled at Sadie. "The police say it was an unfortunate allergic reaction."

"And that's bad for your business." Sadie looked around the room. "You guys, I think we should pray for Miss Clark. She's got a cute store, and she doesn't deserve to have anyone saying bad things about her. I don't know about the rest of you, but I'm gonna stop by Tennessee River Soaps and buy something every time I get paid." A few in the group nodded.

My heart swelled at Sadie's words. "Sadie, that's so sweet of you, but. . ."

"I don't care what people say. I know you wouldn't have hurt her on purpose." Sadie shook her head.

This time I let the students lead in prayer. I bit my lip. *Oh, Lord, what has Sadie heard already?*

Somehow knowing Ben was home but not being able to find him made it worse than when he was hundreds of miles away. I wanted to see his smile, hear his dry jokes, and find out what new snippet of trivia he'd learned on the road. I didn't see him in the crowd at church, although we'd talked on the phone for a few minutes around ten, right after he got to Jackson. Well, he talked, and I ended up dozing off on him. Diana had been right about being tired. I'd dropped off to sleep almost as soon as I returned home the day before.

When I checked my voice mail on the cell phone after church, Ben had called, apologizing for not meeting me at our usual spot in the foyer. He'd been delayed in Jackson, and he expected to return to Greenburg on Monday.

My heart gave a twinge as I headed out into the humidity of the parking lot. I decided to drop in on Momma and Daddy for Sunday dinner. Usually if Ben was in town on the weekend, we'd go out to eat.

Sometimes I wondered why Ben didn't just get his own place. But he always said he didn't need much, just a warm place to come home to. Jerry had a cleaning lady come in once a week, and the bachelors lived a quiet life.

Today, though, I had to see Momma and Daddy and feel the embrace of the familiar. Maybe I still needed to heal up from what I'd witnessed the day before. I considered looking up Melinda's number and calling her but decided against it. Her phone and her parents' phone had probably rung off the wall the entire day and night.

When I tried to imagine losing a sibling, I didn't have to think too hard. Years ago, Momma lost her own sister, my aunt Jewel. Rumor had it that Aunt Jewel ran away the night she turned eighteen. Momma was twenty-three, married, pregnant with Diana. I was a nosy little five-year-old who reeled at the family's grief over my aunt's disappearance. The sensation of loss from yesterday settled around me again.

I let the wind tug at my hair as the Jeep accelerated along Route 64 and headed west out of town. Sun sparkled off the water below the Tennessee River Bridge. Somehow the morose mood that tried to cling to my shoulders blew off and tumbled onto the road behind me.

After turning off the highway onto a back road and then onto my parents' drive, I saw my old home nestled against the edge of the pines. Daddy had built the glorified shotgun shack, room by room, the whole time we were growing up. They added the second story after he retired. Momma's potted plants hung from the front porch and swayed gently in the breeze, as if welcoming me. Miles from town, the peace of my parents' land helped me breathe easier.

Bark lived up to his name as he ran out to meet the Jeep. I pulled up next to Diana and Steve's SUV parked in the red mud driveway.

Momma came out the back door. She wore an apron over her Sunday dress, and her salt-and-pepper hair still retained its weekly set, her one beauty indulgence. "It *is* you! I was just tellin' your daddy I thought I saw you coming up the lane. Where's Ben?"

I climbed out of the driver's seat and shrugged. "He had to wait for a part in Jackson."

She made a noise that sounded like a cross between a harrumph and a grunt right before she hugged me. "Y'all should be married and having a family."

I beat her to her favorite line instead of giving my usual protest. "I know, I'm not getting any younger. But let's not talk about that right now. I'm just glad to be home today."

Momma put her arm around me as we headed to the house. She strolled. I sidestepped the leftover puddles from a recent rainstorm. We climbed the steps and went inside to the kitchen. The TV roared from the front room. Daddy must have a movie on. I pictured him already asleep in his recliner.

"Diana and Steve are taking a walk, and the boys are watching a show with your daddy." Momma shook her head and went to turn the tomatoes frying on the stove. "I can't believe it. That poor Charla Thacker, and right in your store."

"Oh, Momma. It was awful." I settled onto the nearest empty chair at the table. My stomach growled. Someone had already set the table. A mound of potato salad in a bowl, cucumber salad, a tray of pickles, fresh rolls, and the lone health food of tossed salad waited. Forget no-carb, low-carb, good-carb today. I helped myself to an empty glass and poured some sweet tea from the pitcher next to the cucumber salad. *Thank You, Lord, for comfort food.*

"And what a shame. Right before the wedding, too." Momma pointed to the paper towels at the other end of the counter. "Hand me those, hon, so I can lay a few on a clean plate."

Once I fetched the paper towels, I hovered close by the frying pan. I noted a bottle of canola oil next to the stove. No trans fat but still fat. My mouth watered at the thought of the fried green tomatoes.

"Charla had lots of plans." I reached for a still-sizzling fried tomato. "Ouch."

"That'll teach you." Momma grinned and added another few tomatoes to the plate. "We can make all the plans we want, but we don't always know what's coming around the next bend in the road."

"One of my students said something interesting in Sunday school. She said she heard someone say it was about time Charla got a taste of her own medicine." My face grew warm, and it wasn't because of standing next to a hot stove. Momma had taught us not to tale bear, and here I was doing it right in her own kitchen. But there were some things I just had to know.

"Jealousy is a creature that's as ugly as homemade sin." Momma dipped a few sliced tomatoes into egg, rolled them in the flour mixture, and placed them into the hot oil. "Its long-forked tongue never stops moving, and it's got roots like crabgrass. Just when you have it dug out, here it comes sproutin' up again."

I didn't say anything. I hadn't known Charla well. Enough to know she was spoiled, larger than life, and the kind of person you remembered once you met her. I could see how someone would be jealous of that. I tried not to bristle inwardly at recalling the high-and-mighty way she'd treated me. And honestly, I never *wanted* blond hair, either. Too much of a stigma. I'd keep my light brown hair, thank you very much.

No fooling Momma, though. "Didn't really care for her, did you?"

"I'd have to say, honestly, she's probably not someone I'd hang out with. So, um, not exactly." I helped myself to a cooled fried green tomato.

Momma checked the tomatoes and turned them. "I know. I've heard some things about her, too. The blow-dryer at the beauty shop doesn't drown out voices very well. Those ladies blame her for taking their men and leaving a string of broken hearts from here to Memphis."

"What?" Oh, but the tomatoes were good—tangy and sweet and crunchy. Ben had bought me an elliptical trainer for Christmas. I'd have to dust it off and use it.

"Maybe I'm sayin' too much." Momma looked me in the eye. "Just remember, lovin' and leavin's a two-way street. There's more than one side to every story."

My stomach got the sensation it does when my empathy meter starts to kick in. The image of Charla, laughing with her friends, swam into my head. Had her heart been broken, too? I wanted to beg and plead and drag the details out of Momma, but her propriety would make her close up tighter than Fort Knox.

Momma scooped the tomatoes out of the oil and put them to drain on another plate. "You're putting on someone's shoes for a walk, aren't you?"

I nodded. "Whether I want to or not. I know how Charla must have felt." I snatched a fresh paper towel, loaded it up with a few of the cooler tomatoes, and sat back down at the table. Momma understood my empathy. I think she had a bit of that gift herself.

"You're right to think about how Charla Thacker felt, both envied and despised by others." Momma washed her hands before pouring herself a glass of tea. She took a seat across from me.

"I know she was probably frustrated," I said around a bite of tomato. "You can't always control what people think about you, or if they talk about you."

"Just remember that when you're misunderstood."

"Momma, people are already starting to talk about the store. I'd hate it if people didn't come around. I don't know what to do." Momma stood up and moved around the table and put her arms around me. The gesture reminded me of when I was small, and I leaned my head on her apron.

"Do? Hon, you just keep doing. Hold your head high and go about your business. Don't pretend like nothing happened. So long as you know the truth, that's all that matters."

Momma released me and went to check on the chicken in the oven. I pondered her words. "Truth?" Like Pontius Pilate asked, "What is truth?" Or in my case, what is the truth of the matter with Charla Thacker? Sadie's words came back, along with Momma's philosophizing about jealousy. Highly improbable, but not impossible, that someone tampered with the cherry scrub.

I decided then to draft Diana to help me. Once she and Steve returned from their walk, I'd ask her to accompany me to the funeral on Monday. No one was a better people watcher than Di. And working in the bank, she knew plenty about people around town. Maybe nothing would come of the venture, and if so, fine. I needed to pay my respects to the family, and I wasn't brave enough to do it alone. Better to show up at a public place instead of at their front door.

I also reminded myself that jealousy wasn't grounds to accuse someone of murder. If it was, they'd have to lock a lot of us up.

The aromas radiated from a multitude of cooked pasta dishes and hung in the air while the crowded church hall buzzed with a life of its own. Around here, when you bring on the food, you bring on the people. It doesn't matter who dies. Everyone shows up for the after-funeral potluck buffet at First Community Church, the largest house of worship in town.

"Have you ever seen anyone laid out so beautifully?" I heard someone say.

I nearly choked on my bite of shrimp cocktail and grabbed Di's arm. "Did you hear that?"

Di clapped me on the back. "Yes, and by the look of things, Charla's headed for a nomination for sainthood."

One end of the church reception hall had been dedicated to a photo montage of the life of Charla Rae Thacker, who'd been struck down "before her life really began," as someone put it. Easels lined the edge of the room. One poster-size print bore a picture of Charla's graduation from Greenburg High. Another was a candid shot of Charla, with a wide grin and wild blond waves, as she worked with some inner-city Memphis children the summer after her senior year. There was a picture of her and her fiancé, Robert, vacationing on a tropical beach. Another enlarged photo showed Charla swinging a hammer for a Helping Hands Homes project. Whoever put this display together must have used lightning speed with such short notice.

I looked for the owner of the voice that claimed the view of Charla was beautiful. Honey Haggerty. Now that explained the remark. The owner of Honey's Place, Greenburg's best down-home cooking, never shrank from speaking her mind, or using hair coloring so vivid you could see her four blocks away. Now *that* I could envy. Not the hair, but not being concerned with what other people thought.

"You've got to admit, though, the Warners did a great job of making Charla look, um. . ." I couldn't believe I was agreeing with Honey's blaring comment, but I still couldn't forget the sight of Charla's face just before the EMS worker covered it with a sheet.

"Presentable?" Di munched on a carrot stick.

I nodded. "It was so awful to see her that day. We've got to mingle and see if anyone might have had reason to get rid of her."

"Andi, I think you're grasping at air here. How could someone have put something in your scrub?" Di gave a discreet wave to one of her coworkers from the bank.

"One thing at a time, Watson." I took a bite of someone's macaroni-and-cheese surprise, chewed, and swallowed. "We find who, and then we find how."

"Isn't that backwards? Don't the cops usually find evidence first?"

I shrugged. "They've got the evidence, remember? They just don't know it yet. I'm trying to find out who had it in for Charla. Take half the single women in this room, for instance."

"Really, could you tone it down a smidge?" Di shot me a look. I hadn't meant for my tone to rival Honey's.

"Sorry." My face flamed. I checked my cell phone to make sure I had it set on Low. Ben was due back from Jackson, and I didn't want to miss his call. "I say we split up now before my mouth runs away. Then we leave and talk in the car and compare notes."

"Okay, Sherlock." Di grinned and headed off to the bank crew.

I, for one, wanted another glass of sweet tea, so I headed for the drink table and surveyed the room as I crossed it. If I made a list of Charla's victims of the heart, it might be pretty long. But most ladies who'd lost their men to Charla had gone on with their lives. Who would nurse a grudge strong enough to kill? Was it premeditated? Or an impulsive crime of passion?

"That fancy face scrub did it," someone's murmuring voice said as I passed a circle of mourners. I tried not to look and, instead, let their respectfully dark clothing remain a blur.

"And she showed up today. Well, I'll give her points for that."

"Murderers often attend their victims' funerals."

"Oh, come on, it's not like she tried to murder the girl."

Ouch.

I did catch one suspicious glance and wanted to find a place to hide. Fast. I glanced at the food table and stepped up the pace.

Melinda Thacker nearly collided with me as she balanced her loaded plate on one hand and held a cup in the other. Her pale skin contrasted with the black dress she wore, her walnut tresses caught back in a chignon.

I braced my hand gently on the edge of her plate. "I'm sorry, excuse me."

Her eyes widened. "Ms. Clark. Thanks. . .thanks for comin'." Now her eyes glistened. "I've had time to think, and I have to say I was hard on you the other day when. . ."

"Don't worry about it." I touched Melinda's shoulder. "We had a horrible shock, on what should have been a special day for you—and for her." Words failed me, and my mouth went dry. I glanced over her shoulder as a man in a tailored dark suit approached from behind her.

Robert, Charla's fiancé, paused. His arm went around Melinda, and for a second she leaned against him. He murmured in her ear before he moved on. Melinda's face flushed as she flicked her gaze back to me.

Melinda composed herself and blinked. "What almost cracks me up today is knowing that a lot of people here couldn't stand her. They're just here for the show. Maybe they think she deserved what she got. And you know something? She said she knew people hated her, and she was sorry for them."

I had no idea what to add to the conversation. "Charla was larger than life. I think maybe some people hated that. Jealous."

"You're right." Melinda sighed. "People can look you in the eye, say one thing, and mean something else."

"I know. People can be so fake sometimes." I frowned. If I didn't know better, I'd have thought Melinda and I were old friends, and she was speaking to me like a trusted confidant.

Swallow your own prejudice, girl, and be Melinda's friend. Maybe that's what Melinda needed. A true friend. The neediness radiating from her practically bowled me over. Regardless of Thacker money or social status, I wouldn't let the idea of me being a lowly Clark keep me from crossing that bridge and reaching out to the bereaved young woman.

One of the women from Melinda's church appeared at her elbow, and I heard the soft chimes of my cell phone from the depths of my bag.

"Melinda, I'll call you—"

"Okay. I'd. . .like that. Take care now, you hear?" With her parting words, Melinda turned and released me from her intense expression.

I moved to the trash can, tossed away my half-eaten food, and wished for Momma's cooking. Once I sat my tea glass on the edge of the drink table, I fished out my phone.

"Ben, where are you?"

"I'm almost home." Static hissed in my ears.

"Hang on, let me go into the hallway."

"Where are you? At a party? Without me?" His voice sounded plaintive.

"Ha. No." I pushed through the door that led to the hallway of restrooms. "I'm at the potluck for Charla Thacker."

"Well, I'll come and rescue you once I get home and shower. I have something important to talk to you about." I didn't miss his serious tone. It made my throat hurt.

The hallway echoed with the sound of my footsteps taking me to the ladies' room. "What's that?"

"Don't worry, it's good."

"Now you've got me wonderin'."

"That's the idea. I love you, babe."

"I love you, too. See you soon." I flipped my phone shut and sighed. We might be Greenburg's longest-running dating couple—well, second-longest if you count Honey Haggerty and Junker Joe Toms, and even they've probably given up on the idea of marriage—but Ben's voice still set my heart pounding. Several different possibilities sprang to mind about what Ben wanted to discuss.

Ben planned. I had loose ideas about what I wanted to happen. The idea of the next fifty years of my life, already decided? *Lord, what's wrong with me?* I knew I shouldn't be afraid to say "I do" to Ben.

Was I still holding out for someone more polished, more ambitious? Ridiculous. And then I thought of my parents. Daddy had fallen short in his career. Some nights I saw the traces of his regret when we looked at the constellations or a new moon through his telescope. An injury had knocked him out of the navy too early and dashed his dreams of being a flight engineer. He'd settled for working up and down the Mississippi. Good money, but the grease under his fingernails still made his job not good enough for some in Greenburg.

Momma was proud of him. Yet I wondered sometimes if she regretted never seeing the sights she always dreamed of. She still had the kitchen decorated with pictures of Paris and Rome and other places she wanted to visit.

"One day," Momma would say. I understood the restless feeling. One day I, too, wanted to see and do things bigger than Greenburg. Maybe that's why although I loved the store, I felt the pull toward something else. Ben seemed content in his pattern.

I entered the bathroom. Another woman was washing her hands at the sink, but other than that, the place seemed empty. She dried her hands, and the door gave a drawn-out, plaintive squeak as she left.

The mirror told me I needed to reapply some lipstick. I fumbled with the tube and my cell phone. The phone won, and the tube clattered to the floor and rolled, clicking its way along the tiles and into an empty stall.

My tube of Mocha Bliss had cost eight fifty at Walgreen's. That's almost a Charla Thacker kind of price in Greenburg, so I wasn't about to let it go. Reminding myself that a refrigerator can hold more bacteria than a bathroom floor, I entered the stall and let the door bang shut behind me.

The tube taunted me from where it lay at the edge of the wall. I tried to stretch to see if I could reach it.

Then I tried to get my leg in between the toilet and wall, but my backside wouldn't let me. Okay, now for the squat and reach—

And that's when the door to the bathroom creaked open, and a pair of female voices floated in on the air.

"I'm just about done tryin' to look real sad," one voice began.

"Oh, don't you know it?" Heels clacked on the tile floor. My back cramped, but I snatched the lipstick anyway.

Someone turned on the faucet. I could still hear over the rush of water. "I wish we could all take a microphone and say, 'Now here's the *real* Charla Thacker! This was *her* life!'" The voice rang against the walls. "Funny, they don't have a poster of when we were shoplifting buddies in high school."

"Shush, do you want someone to hear you?" The faucet went off, and I heard the ripping of paper towels. I could scarcely breathe. Should I betray my presence and embarrass them? I know I'd be embarrassed if someone overheard me slinging thoughts like that around like yesterday's garbage.

"Don't tell me lots of people wouldn't agree with me."

"That's not the point. She died a week before her wedding."

"Robert would have been mine if she hadn't paraded in front of him and played the helpless female." The trash can lid clicked. "Trying to sue Mike Chandler. Yeah, right."

"Aren't you and Jared happy?"

"We are, but all I can say is, you give out ugly, and you get it right back one day."

The quieter it got, the more my back hurt, but no way was I getting up or releasing my hold on Mocha Bliss.

"Stop it. Your hair looks fine. No one's going to notice if it's messed up."

"Humph. They're all *still* looking at Charla. Those posters are big enough to choke someone."

The clacking heels announced the women's exit as did the squeaking door. I stood up and groaned. Things had just gotten a whole lot more interesting. Then it dawned on me that I needed to find out about those speakers. Like their names, perhaps. And what was that about suing Mike Chandler? The guy ran his family produce farm outside town.

I slipped from the bathroom stall and tiptoed to the door. Maybe if I pulled the door handle slowly, the hinges wouldn't announce themselves. Once I'd opened it about six inches, I peeked out the door.

All I caught was a glimpse of the hem of a dark skirt and someone's nice, dressy slingbacks before the door to the main hall closed. So, who was the bitter woman dating Jared? I needed to ask Di.

"The only Jared I know of sells cars over at MidRiver Motors." Di and I stood by her van in the church parking lot, where we took a moment to regroup without being overheard. "He and Kaitlyn—oh, I can't remember her last name—have been seeing each other for about six months. I don't really know her, but someone mentioned something at work while some of us were at the coffeepot. I tried not to listen, but now with what happened to Charla, I can't help but remember."

I squinted at the bright sky and wished I'd brought my sunglasses. "Six months, you say. Well, she doesn't sound like a murderer. I have a feeling that if we check out every person Charla made jealous—or who knows what—we'd spend a lot of time spinning our wheels and getting nowhere. Maybe we should check out her recent past or see who had the biggest grudge."

"We could. It sounds like Kaitlyn's still pretty miffed about what happened, even though she's moved on. And Robert Robertson sounds like he was quite an item himself." Di shook her head.

"I wonder if Kaitlyn nursed a secret grudge. Maybe she wanted to be the one on the way to the altar." I pondered the idea. Where did someone cross the line from being bitter to becoming a murderer?

"Would you just listen to us?" Di's voice squeaked. "People have private lives, and quite frankly I'd hate it if someone suspected me of murder just because I had a grudge. I didn't mind coming with you today, because you definitely needed the moral support, but—"

"You draw the line at us being the Hardy Girls."

"It's Hardy *Boys*. I started reading them to Taylor and Stevie."

"I know what they're called." My stomach churned,

my new shoes had chafed my heels, and I felt downright cranky. "This is my *business* we're talking about. If someone sabotaged that cherry facial scrub, I've got to know. Because I know it wasn't me. So, did *you* learn anything?"

Di shook her head. "Not really. I'm not as nosy as you are."

"Oh, isn't that nice of you to say?"

"I didn't mean it like that. I'm not good at asking those kinds of questions. I probably wouldn't know a clue if it ran up and bit me." She lifted her hands, palms up. "I tried. I only noticed how sad the Thackers are."

The parking lot still had plenty of cars, which probably meant the food supply was still holding up. "We ought to go back in. When else will we have so many potential suspects in one room?"

Di gave a soft chuckle. "You sound full of sympathy."

"I am, actually." We started walking back to the door that led to the church reception hall. "Even though the Thackers might not believe or suspect their daughter died because of foul play, they deserve to know the truth if I can find it. That's the least I can do for them."

"Why you, though?"

"Why not me?" I pulled the door open and felt a blast of cool air from the reception hall. Yes, going inside was definitely better than sweltering outside. "I can't sit by and do nothing. If it turns out I'm wrong, that's all right."

"Hello, Mrs. Mann." Di smiled at a woman wearing a dark pantsuit. She nodded and pushed past us to leave, the heavy door closing behind her.

My eyes adjusted to the muted lighting, and I tried to find at least one of the women I'd heard in the bathroom. "Do you see Kaitlyn? I know one of them had some black slingbacks, and one wore a dark skirt."

Suddenly it seemed as though all the women wore dark skirts, now that Mrs. Mann had left the building. I couldn't very well stare at everyone's feet until I found the right person. And once again, what would I say if I came face-to-face with her? "I'm not sure who she is. Maybe I can ask one of the girls from the bank." Di frowned. "Although they'd wonder why. . . . See, I told you I'm not good at asking questions."

"That's okay. Do me a favor. See if anyone's wearing a pair of black slingbacks."

"I can do that. Um, what are slingbacks?" Di studied the footwear of everyone who passed by. We stood next to the trash can like a couple of waifs.

"They're high-heeled sandals with a buckle and a thin strap across the back of the ankle. Although I bet everyone shopped at Payless this year." I glanced at one woman's black skirt. No, that was a broomstick skirt with a crinkled texture. The other skirt I'd seen looked more tailored. This was ridiculous, scrutinizing everyone's wardrobe. "Stay here. I'll be right back."

I headed to Trudy, the wearer of the broomstick skirt and owner of Higher Grounds coffee shop. She looked as uncomfortable as I felt. "Hi there."

"Hey, Andi. Wasn't that a beautiful service?" Her long, dark hair hung in a braid over one shoulder.

I nodded. "Have you seen Kaitlyn anywhere?"

"Kaitlyn Branch?"

"I guess that might be her last name." I didn't think I was very good at bluffing, but I smiled as I spoke to the caffeine maven of Greenburg.

"She's over there, talking to Robert Robertson." Trudy gestured with her head.

"Thanks." Normally I'd have stayed with Trudy and helped her bear her discomfort, but I at least wanted to speak to Kaitlyn and see what information I could glean.

Some people don't talk to strangers. Others confess to strangers matters they'd never divulge to their best friend. I was counting on Kaitlyn being the latter type of person.

Fortunately, Robert and Kaitlyn stood next to the food table. I couldn't catch their conversation, but neither looked happy. Of course, it wasn't like today's events called for an occasion of rejoicing.

Even though the table looked like a locust plague had already descended on the food spread from one end to the other, I grabbed a fresh paper plate and tried to find something palatable to put on it. Momma would scold me for taking food I didn't intend to eat. Truth be told, I *liked* corn casserole, enough to try to find out who made it and get the recipe, which said a lot for church buffet food.

"Sorry about what happened. . ." Kaitlyn's soft tones dripped with sympathy. She touched the sleeve of Robert's suit jacket and gave him a sad smile that oozed with much more than sympathy. I glanced at her feet. Yep, slingbacks.

He nodded, his eyelids blinking rapidly. "I can't believe she's gone. It's like I'm stuck in a nightmare." I forced myself to look away and instead studied the nearest giant picture—of Charla on horseback.

"If you ever need to talk, I'm here."

"I don't think I'll need to talk. At least not to you." Robert's voice rasped as though he had laryngitis.

"I'm just trying to help," Kaitlyn hissed. At that, I ventured a glance in their direction. Then I snapped my gaze to a bowl that held a tablespoon of green bean casserole.

"I don't need your help." He darted sideways and almost ran into me. "Excuse me," he said as he made his getaway.

Kaitlyn stood like a lost little girl in a crowd, so I seized my chance. "I'm sorry, I couldn't help but overhear. Are you all right?"

She blinked hard as she looked my way. "I'll be fine. It's hard for me to see him like that. He was always so together, larger than life, and now. . ."

"What a tragedy, and right before their wedding, too." I shook my head. "Did you know Charla well?"

"I knew her well enough." A hardness made Kaitlyn's jaw look like granite. "Some people are larger than life, even after they die." Her expression focused behind me, and I glanced back at the poster display.

"That's something else, isn't it?" I was running out of small talk ideas, and the crowd was beginning to dwindle. Di looked stranded next to the trash can. She clutched a paper cup and kept giving me looks that said she was ready to drag me from the building. I ignored her and faced Kaitlyn.

"You know what? See that picture of the inner-city project in Memphis?" Kaitlyn leaned closer. "She only showed up one afternoon, complained about everything, and never came back after that. Sure made out like a fat rat, shopping while the rest of us worked."

"Oh. I suppose things aren't always as they seem." The joy with which Kaitlyn tainted the public display amazed me.

"Did I hear someone mention something about Charla suing somebody?" Every Proverb I'd ever read about talebearers flitted through my brain.

Kaitlyn pounced on this tidbit. "You're right. She tried to sue Mike Chandler. Said he tried to poison her. The case got thrown out, though."

"Really?" I've never taken acting classes, but for this performance, I'd have gotten an A. I saw Di pull out her cell phone and take a call after she shot me a glare, mouthing, "Let's go."

"Hey, baby." A lanky young man with a trimmed beard, wearing a striped shirt and a too-long tie, sidled up to Kaitlyn. Her smile didn't hold nearly the same brilliance as the one she'd given Robert, the grieving fiancé.

"Hi." She received the kiss on the cheek he gave her and took his hand. "This is Jared."

"Oh, um, hello." Di was walking our way—

"Andi, I hate to break the news to you, but I've got to go." Di glanced down at her watch. "The babysitter has to leave, and I already owe her more than I budgeted."

"Kaitlyn, Jared, nice chatting with you." I still held my plate of uneaten food. "Take care, now."

The last thing I heard as I walked away was Kaitlyn saying, "Who was that? And how'd she know my name?"

Okay, I never said I was much good as a sleuth, but I had to start somewhere. Next stop, Mike Chandler. I had to find out about that lawsuit. If he was miffed about it, maybe he'd talk.

Back into the humid afternoon we went and headed to Di's van. I climbed into the passenger seat. "Sorry about that."

Di started the van and cranked the air-conditioning up to full blast. "Don't worry about it. Did you learn anything interesting?"

"As a matter of fact, I did. Charla accused Mike Chandler of trying to poison her once out of revenge."

"Wow."

"That was my reaction. I was hoping to get Kaitlyn to tell me more about it, but her boyfriend came up. . ."

"And so did I. Sorry."

"Don't worry about it. I can accomplish two things when I go to Chandler's Farmer's Market. Get some strawberries so Ben and I can have strawberry shortcake, and ask Mike a few questions." As we pulled out of the church parking lot, I told her how I'd blown it by calling Kaitlyn by name when she hadn't introduced herself.

Di laughed. "She probably had no clue how you knew her, anyway. Say, is Ben home yet?"

"Almost."

"Do you want me to drop you off at his place or at home?"

"Home. I need to change out of these dressy clothes." Nylons and humidity definitely do *not* mix.

At the sight of Ben's navy blue tractor rig in the driveway of his and Jerry's house, I felt better already. I was soon up the stairs and standing at the door. My heart pounded.

Then, the door opened, and without a word, Ben pulled me into his arms. I breathed in a hint of cologne and the scent of his freshly washed hair. He'd been working out while on the road, using the resistance bands I'd bought him for his birthday. He wore a blue pullover shirt I didn't remember seeing before, something that he'd normally wear to church and not on a Monday afternoon. His kiss reminded me of why getting married would be a *very* good idea. But—

"I missed you," Ben murmured into my ear, his voice gravelly.

I stepped back but still remained in his arms. "I missed you, too. It was awful not having you here with everything that was going on." Ben made up for our two weeks apart with another kiss.

When he held me at arm's length, his blue eyes were twinkling. "Well, I'm here now, and you can tell me about it when we get back."

"Back from where?"

His face took on an unreadable expression. "Somewhere. I have a surprise for you."

"Okay. Where are we going?" I tried to block his path down the stairs but figured he might try to tote me over his shoulder like he did once before when I got sassy (as he claimed) and got in his way.

"You'll see." He took a step closer, and I reconsidered trying to make a human barrier at the top of the stairs.

We headed to my Jeep, where I tossed him the keys. He backed out down the driveway.

"You get the oil changed on this yet?" Ben shifted into first gear.

"I was going to. . . . Been kind of busy lately."

He reached for my hand once we were on the main road going into town. "I'll take care of it before I leave again."

I kept my questions to myself and instead filled him in on my and Diana's efforts at the after-funeral dinner. "I know someone had it in for Charla Thacker, probably enough to kill her."

Ben shook his head. "I don't get it, though. Why go through all that trouble? It seems like a hassle to get into your store and sabotage the scrub."

"Which is why I think whoever did this had more

than just a jealous snit. It was in cold blood." I sighed.

We made it through Greenburg's half a dozen traffic lights that stayed green for us all the way.

"Um, we're not heading to my parents' house, are we?"

"Nope. Before that." Ben slowed once we passed a grove of pines, then downshifted and turned into an overgrown driveway.

I'd been by this empty lot more times than I could imagine in the past years. Now I noticed a small real estate sign with a red and white SOLD sticker plastered across it.

"Did you?"

Ben's chest puffed out. "I bought it. Ten acres, and the back part of the acreage ends near the river. This was Doris Flanders's property. I got it for a good price. I wish the old house was still here."

Ben is not known for his long speeches. He is a man who communicates more through his eyes and his hands and his posture. His eyebrows seem to speak, too. And now his words puzzled me.

"You bought this?" The gently rolling property needed some upkeep, but there might be a good spot for a garden by the rickety wooden shed across the driveway from the empty building lot. I glimpsed a few young watermelons studding the green vines that stretched from the end of the drive all the way to the shed.

"Isn't it great?" Ben caressed my hand. "I've decided it's time to set down roots of my own. Jerry and I get along fine, but I need my own space. My own roots. This land's a start. One day a house. No hurry, though."

I tried to take a deep breath, but my lungs didn't seem to want to fill with air. Roots might as well have been ropes, tying me to the ground. This confirmed the nightmare I'd had one night of racing through a field, laughing with Ben. Then giant roots came snaking out of the ground and grabbed me like a boa constrictor. How could I tell him these things, with him sitting there looking as if he'd just won the lottery?

5

On Tuesday morning, I drove to Tennessee River Soaps. My heart dragged behind me all the way. Somehow I had to force myself to go through the motions of opening the shop, working on fresh product, and drumming up business before the whole operation went south. I thought of poor Charla and the fact that Greenburg was going to have to figure out how to get along without her. I hadn't known her well, but what had her death done to those who did?

I drove into the parking lot and slammed on the brakes again. Not because someone had broken into the store, though.

Instead, someone had scrawled KILLER across the plate-glass window. I clamped my hand over my mouth. The glaring red letters obscured the pretty logo with its blue and green motifs that swirled around brown lettering. Diana and I had spent hours painting the glass one spring day. I had cried then when I realized my dream was coming true. I wanted to cry now at the thought of my dream turning into a nightmare.

Was the vandalism worth calling Jerry about? I sighed, not wanting to add to his workload. I turned off the Jeep, left it parked kitty-corner in the lot, and trudged to the front window. A corner of the *K* flaked off easily. Soap pen?

Someone wasn't making a heavy-duty threat here.

If they were, they'd have used spray paint.

It took me forty-five minutes to scrub the gunk from the window. As I used a wet cloth to remove the letters, a smear of paint covered my logo. A red smear. *Lord, not a smear on my business.* I kept glancing over my shoulder to see when the first customers would arrive.

It wasn't as if I needed to hold my breath or anything. A full hour after my scheduled opening time, no one had shown up, not even to sample every product and then leave the store without buying anything, as many lookers were wont to do.

I sat down to my second cup of coffee. The scent mingled with the others on the sales floor—fruity, musky, floral. Melinda's face came to mind. I couldn't imagine the heart-numbing pain after losing a sister. Learning to go on after someone died suddenly couldn't be easy. I looked at the phone. I had Melinda's cell phone number from setting up Charla's ill-fated spa party. Maybe now would be the perfect time to call, especially to snap myself out of my pity party. I certainly hadn't known a great loss like Melinda. As I let my gaze wander around the storefront, I realized things can be replaced. I could always find another line of work, but people were irreplaceable.

Melinda answered on the second ring.

"Hi, this is Andi Clark. Um, just thought I'd call and see how you're doing." *Now that was a stupid remark. How do you think she's doing?* I already had one hand on the proverbial shovel, preparing to dig a hole for myself.

"All right, I guess." An infinite weariness drifted across the phone line.

"I know it's probably quiet around there now, with everyone getting back to their routines. I was just thinking about you, and. . ." I closed my mouth and let the words hang between us.

"Thanks. It means a lot for you to call. I just keep expecting the phone will ring and it'll be Charla, saying she's running late. Again. And then I remember."

"I'm. . .I'm really sorry about what happened." My throat caught. "Charla and I were so careful, and I still don't understand. . . ." I considered asking about the lawsuit Charla had brought against Mike Chandler but reconsidered.

Melinda coughed. "I know you were. And I've got to apologize. That day, I said some horrible things. It wasn't your fault." Now she sniffed.

"Don't worry about what you said." I tried to reassure her. "Sometimes we say things when we're really upset, and. . ."

"Listen, I know why you're really calling."

"You do?"

She sniffled again. "I know you feel responsible for that allergic reaction. But now that I look back, Charla was really overdoin' it. She hated being told she couldn't do something. She just never got used to living with food allergies."

"Really?" I tried not to suck in a deep breath. She thought I felt guilty.

"Yeah. Charla liked to push it. Eggs, mangoes,

strawberries, and peanuts. She hated that list when we were kids. But the worst reaction she always had was to anything strawberry." Melinda's voice drifted to a whisper. "Oh. . .I'm rambling. No one's really called since the funeral. It's hard to know what to do besides talk. I'm sorry. I barely know you."

"Don't apologize. Maybe you just needed to vent a little." My mind raced off from the subject at hand. I directed it back to Melinda. "We should meet for lunch sometime, if you want. I don't know if you have anyone else to talk to. . . ."

"I've got friends—but thanks, I might take you up on that. People get busy and get involved with their own lives again." It sounded as though she had pulled the phone away from her ear. "I'm getting another call. Can I let you go?"

"Sure. Bye for now."

I put down the phone and let my mind hit overdrive. *Charla always had the worst reaction to strawberry.* This was common knowledge to those who knew her. And it was a fact anyone could learn. Our town had plenty of loose tongues, and news was news. You could spoon up all kinds of dirt on people if you tried hard enough. I didn't, though, since Momma and Daddy had raised me well enough to know when something wasn't my business. Most of the time. I let out a sigh.

I needed Ben's logic, or maybe it was just the idea of being around him. He let me ramble and think things out all the time. Dear, sweet Ben, who let me finish what I was saying and usually seemed pretty interested in what I had to say. Unlike some men who develop male-pattern deafness.

When I called Ben's cell phone, I got his voice mail and remembered he'd gone to Home Depot for some window shopping. Evidently he was taking this settling-down thing seriously. Once Ben made up his mind, he was a man on a mission. Sometimes, though, he got swept away in his plans and didn't mention them to me. Not like I *had* to give him permission or input. He was just used to being on his own and answering to no one but God.

Back to strawberries again. Somehow strawberry had to have gotten into that scrub. I tried to think of all the forms strawberry could come in. Dried strawberry, essential oil, food flavoring. . . What I needed to do was look at the evidence.

I moved from my perch behind the register and glanced out the front window. The sun beat down on an empty parking lot outside.

Jerry had to know something by now, didn't he? And there was that matter of the message on the window this morning. I had a pretty good reason to call him, so I did.

He sounded flustered when he took my call at his desk. "Andi, I'm up to my eyeballs in work today, but what's going on?"

"I know you're busy, but I won't take long. This morning I was greeted by the word *killer* written in red soap pen on my front store window."

"Is it still there?"

"Um, no, I washed it off."

"Not much I can do about that now. I can file a report."

Duh. "Yes, well. . .I was wondering. Did you get an initial report back on Charla's death? Anything on the facial scrub?"

"You know I can't say right now."

"Jer, I know you're going to release a statement to the paper. If you know something, just tell me what you'd tell them. Do you have a cause of death?"

Jerry sighed. "Anaphylactic shock."

"And my scrub?"

"Still at the lab. Don't know exactly when those results will come back. We've got a cause of death and a signed death certificate, and no crime was committed. So testing your scrub isn't really a priority."

"Well, thanks anyhow."

"No problem."

When I hung up the phone, I felt like I'd bugged him for almost no reason at all.

With a sigh, I turned my back on the summer day and entered the workroom where I made my concoctions.

The large tub of cherry scrub flakes sat where I'd left it on Saturday. Greenburg PD had taken only Charla's scrub from the main room, but all of the product had come from this tub. I grabbed a plastic scoop and started swirling the flakes around. The fruity scent met my nostrils.

I couldn't enjoy the aroma as I normally did. Cherry blossoms, smelling like spring. It had meant death for Charla. Some darkish specks stood out against the pink soap-scrub flakes. What was this? The small nubbins didn't belong in this scrub.

Once I found a clean bowl, I heaped a few generous scoops of scrub into it and pushed the flakes around with my finger. I lifted a palmful to my nose and inhaled.

Cherry. . .and something else. The wild tang also bore a hint of different sweetness. Of strawberries?

I needed a sifter, so I pulled one from the utensil drawer. Maybe these darkish flecks would pass through and leave flakes behind.

A minute later, I'd sifted the flakes until some of the specks covered the table. I licked a finger and grimaced at the soap taste, then dabbed at the specks on the table with my damp finger. I squinted at them, then went to fetch a magnifier from my tool drawer.

There on the worktable. . .strawberry seeds?

My heart pounded and I thought of something else. The break-in on the morning of Charla's party might not have been another in the series of break-ins plaguing the business owners of Greenburg. Ben had voiced—and dismissed—the idea that someone had sabotaged the scrub. Someone knew of Charla's allergy and knew about the party.

Someone who hated her enough to kill her.

Now, more than ever, I had to get to Mike Chandler and find out about that lawsuit, how she said he'd tried to poison her. What if Charla had been right, and what if this time he'd succeeded? I'd have to be careful with my questions.

Another thing. Mike employed his teenage nephews and a few of their friends during the summer. He needed strong workers on the farm. What if one of them had helped him break into the store and put strawberries in the scrub? He certainly had plenty of the sweet deadly fruit in his fields, ripe for picking.

6

"Baby, *murder* is a very strong word." Ben took my hand across our favorite table at Honey's Place. Someone had the music cranked up loud, probably to drown out the Tuesday lunch din, and I had to lean closer to catch Ben's words.

"I still say that break-in was no coincidence, and I'm going to find out who messed with that cherry scrub. I feel like this entire tragedy is partly my fault." Pulling my hand free, I grabbed my fork and jabbed into a piece of hot biscuit. I swirled the biscuit in my side bowl of chocolate gravy, then popped the flaky morsel into my mouth. A swallow of coffee followed the swallow of biscuit. I'd ordered from the breakfast menu. Nothing sweeter than being with Ben at Greenburg's yummiest down-home eatery. I wished our conversation was sweeter.

"You're being too hard on yourself. You had no way of knowing this was going to happen. Because sometimes bad things. . .happen." Ben took a sip of his coffee. "And you need to accept it, like the rain falling on the just and unjust."

I love him more than I can say, but sometimes Ben just doesn't get it. "I know that. And I don't think that's what happened here. I'm going to prove she was murdered, but I don't know how."

"Charla's death was an accident, pure and simple.

You shouldn't shoulder responsibility for that."

"But it happened at my store. Tennessee River Soaps is my livelihood, and I've got to do what I can to show her death wasn't because of my negligence. I've just got to." I tried not to whine, but the last couple of words squeaked out. Good thing the music was loud. People would probably be staring otherwise, and I wasn't about to have a meltdown at Honey's. Such occasions best took place behind closed doors, with much prayer afterward.

"Shh." Ben reached out again for my hand and rubbed the back of it with his thumb. "Don't let this setback keep you down. Things will turn around."

I bit my lip then consoled myself with more of the divine chocolate gravy. After I swallowed, I continued. "I know. I'm not giving up."

Somehow I didn't sound very convincing. I'd only had one customer that morning, and she'd only bought one of the clearance bars of soap after traipsing around the shop for thirty minutes. My eyes blurred with tears.

"Don't get discouraged. You've just got to determine to press on."

"Determination alone won't pay the rent. I need to update the Web site and do some better Internet marketing, but that costs money, too." I could hardly talk around the knot in my throat. Money. I didn't like talking money with Ben, who could make a penny shriek because he pinched it so tight, then was given to unexpected sweet gestures like the topaz bracelet that sparkled on my wrist.

"If you need money, consider me an investor."

"I couldn't—"

"Well, I'm not going to let you give up on this dream." The sunlight coming through the window made Ben's blue eyes gleam. "And before we get into talking about money, don't let pride keep you from following through, either."

"Following through?"

"You just seem. . .like you give up too easily sometimes." He took my other hand. "Because, when you have something worth fighting for, you hang on no matter what." Ben's gaze held me, and the music got swallowed up by the pounding in my ears.

"You're not just talking about the business, are you?"

"No."

"You know I love you, Ben." Had I spoken out loud? Why was saying "I love you" so hard?

"I know." He gave a slight nod. "I love you, too. Which is why I'm committed to seeing us through. Every night I pray I'm the kind of man God wants me to be—for you."

Many women would kill to hear a guy use the words *committed* and *love* in the same sentence. Me? I felt like I was starting to choke. I needed to say something, but my mind only echoed with the twangy song playing over the speakers. At last, the sounds of clanking silverware and the murmurs of diners registered in my ears.

The last few times Ben had come home from the road, he spoke about home. Family. Having a permanent roof over his head. His eyes reflected the future looming between us. Its fingers increased their grip on my throat. . .

"More coffee, sweetie?" Honey appeared at my elbow, snapping me out of my reverie.

"Um, yeah." I tried to grin at her, but I think it came out as a grimace. "Fill 'er up."

"You need a fresh bowl of gravy?" Honey gestured with the coffeepot. "Spendin' all your time talkin' has set yours up to pudding."

"Sure, sure." Although I wasn't sure I could eat anything more.

Honey swirled away with a flash of red hair and white apron. She'd probably forget the gravy, but I knew she wouldn't leave the table until I agreed to the fresh bowl.

"Are you upset with me?" Ben finished the last of his burger.

I shook my head. "It's me." His words made me realize I'd kept him at arm's length while at the same time saying I loved him. "Love means vulnerability, and I. . .I have a hard time being vulnerable."

"Why?" His forehead wrinkled. "I know I've been gone a lot these years, but since I've been with you, no one else makes me feel like coming home. Are you afraid of *me*?"

"No." My response came out in a whisper. "It's not you. Like I said, it's me."

Now the singer in the background was belting out a song about lovin' and leavin'. What a fitting way to fill the silence. I couldn't tell him I wanted to be the one to fly and be free. For a wild moment I almost considered closing the shop and running. *Stop it.*

"When the Lord mentioned He was teachin' me patience through you, He wasn't joking." Ben shook his head.

I gritted my teeth before I replied. "Glad I could help. I can't just wish these feelings away, even if I don't want them."

"That's why I believe in us. Even though there's been times I could've walked away, given in to temptation. . ."

"What?" I hadn't expected this. "What do you mean?" "Don't you think, the line of work I'm in, there are lonely women wanting to spend time with a man who'll be gone the next day? Temptation makes some drivers cave. But not all of us. And not me."

I squirmed in the booth. No one beat down my door while Ben was gone. But Ben had a likability about him, the kind of guy mothers love and who makes their daughters laugh, and the kind that other guys would trust to run the barbecue grill. He didn't spend much time in town, and when he did, we were together.

"If you wanted to be free, you could have said something a long time ago."

"That's not what I want. I'm free with you, Andi Clark."

"And yet I try your patience."

"You're worth waiting for."

"I'm glad you think so." *Lord, I don't deserve his sweetness*. Few people in my life could tell me the unembellished truth without leaving me licking my wounds. Still, though, it did sting. "It's not that I can't commit or I don't want to. Feelings are hard to change. Like I said." *But give up too easily?*

"I love you just the way you are, feelings and all."

"Thanks." What else could I say? Well-intentioned people like him and Di always tried to tell me what I already knew, and I didn't want to be controlled. I didn't tell him that though.

"I'm leaving Friday. I should be back in ten days." Ben wiped his mouth with his napkin. His expression had sealed itself off again. Men like Ben don't love halfway, and I felt like a fraud for my silence.

I nodded. "I'll miss you."

"Are you mad about me offering money, or me saying that you give up too easily?"

"No, I'm not mad about you wanting to help. Really. Sometimes the truth hurts." I blinked hard, not wanting to tear up.

Ben took the check that Honey had deposited after dropping off our meals, and he stood. He extended his hand in my direction.

For some reason half a dozen tables of customers had decided to leave Honey's en masse and were waiting in line to pay their checks.

Feeling like a world-class idiot, I stood beside Ben and waited. I wanted to run outside but forced myself to wait in line. A voice that dripped with bitterness made me turn. Especially when the name "Charla Thacker" met my ears.

Mike Chandler and a few of his buddies were divvying up their check before they arrived at the register.

"I wish I could have been there to see that." He ground out the words as I stared back at them. "She never wanted a hair out of place, acted like it was the end of the world if the wind kicked up."

"Man, that's cold," one of his buddies commented. "Why would you want to watch her die?"

"Cold?" His voice rose, and now I wasn't the only one staring. "You know why she broke up with me? She didn't like the sound of the name Charla Chandler, and she decided she didn't want to be tied down to a farmer."

"I don't get it. What's the big deal?"

"She almost put me out of business last summer. Said I tried to poison her with strawberries. Ironic that she died of an allergic reaction. Served her right. Like I said, part of me wished I could have seen that."

Ben's touch on my hand made me whirl back around. We moved up in line. I sucked in a breath at Mike's words. He had intense brown eyes and a goatee and rarely smiled, but he'd just spoken more than I'd ever heard him say in all the years I'd stopped by Chandler's Farmer's Market.

I took a deep breath, then leaned forward and whispered at Ben. "Hey."

He half turned in line. "Hey, what?"

"Mike just said Charla accused him of trying to poison her last summer. . .with strawberries."

"Baby, stop." Ben stepped up to the counter and handed our check to the woman at the register who would somehow make sense of Honey's scribbles and numbers.

"Stop what?"

"You can't accuse people of murder just by over-heard conversations."

"You heard?"

Ben's eyes glinted as he looked at me. "I heard a few things. I figured I'd mind my own business and not listen."

"I'm not a busybody."

"Nobody said you were." We walked into the blaze of summer outside, damp with humidity and making good on the weatherman's promise of a mid-June scorcher.

Ben pulled me close once we'd stopped at his truck. "I'm leaving soon. Think you could pay me a little attention?" His dimples came out and coaxed me to relax in his arms.

"I think so."

He leaned in for a quick kiss. A car's honk made me spring back, my face flaming. Why did I go from feeling strangled to never wanting him to let me go? *Lord, I could really use some help with this one. Di oughta be good for some advice.*

"I'll miss you." My throat caught.

"I'll be home again before you know it." Ben gave

me another hug. "I have a feeling my days on the road are numbered. So don't give up on us."

"I won't." I smiled at him. "And I won't give up trying to find out how someone tried to kill Charla Thacker."

Ben groaned and shook his head then kissed me again.

"Madam, your books are done—in under twenty minutes." Di snapped the Tennessee River Soaps ledger closed and grinned. My sister has this sick love affair with numbers, which is why I paid her to do my books—so I could feel free to be creative. Although today I felt anything but creative as I looked at my showroom floor brimming with inventory.

"Don't look so happy." I sank onto the stool behind the counter. "If business was better, you'd be taking longer." As it was, my Saturday morning rush had already come and gone. All two of them.

"Wish you were paying me by the hour?"

I shrugged. My stomach growled, too soon for lunch.

"What is it?" She leaned closer. "What's wrong?"

We have a unique role reversal, my sister Diana and me. Her listening heart helped me through my rocky teen years and young adulthood, and I helped her not take herself too seriously.

I sipped my coffee and sighed. "Remember when I suspected someone tried to murder Charla by sabotaging my facial scrub? Well, now I'm sure of it. And I'm sure the lab is going to take forever on testing the scrub, since Charla's death was ruled an accident. But after what I heard Mike Chandler spew at Honey's the other day, I'm going to start looking around on my own."

I outlined the whole scenario for her, from finding the strawberry seeds in the scrub, to hearing Mike at Honey's. Like Ben, Di let me ramble on, only punctuating my story with a few sympathetic "ummhmm's." Her eyebrows would have shot to the ceiling had they not been firmly attached to her forehead.

"Wow." She started to pace the store. "So, let's put on our Hardy Girls' caps again."

"I thought you didn't want to be the Hardy Girls."

"I changed my mind after this latest development. From what you said, Mike's not someone who's merely disgruntled, but someone who seemed genuinely tickled pink that Charla died." Di strode past me and into the back office. Her voice trailed to the front. "Okay, we'll make a list of suspects." She emerged with paper and pen, then hopped onto the stool next to mine.

"First, we list the bridesmaids. Hang on, I've got the list from Charla's party." Now it was my turn to trot back and forth from the office. "Here it is. . .Melinda, Emily, Tess, Mitchalene. And the fiancé, Robert. He's not on the list, but he knew about the party. Put Mike down, too."

Di jotted on the paper. "What about that woman you heard in the bathroom after the funeral?"

"Kaitlyn, in the slingbacks. . ." My stomach turned. "I don't know. She sounded more bitter than murderous."

"I'm adding her to the list anyway." Di studied the ceiling as if it would help her remember the woman's name. "Kaitlyn. . ."

"Branch." I shrugged. "She didn't have access or immediate knowledge of the spa party. . .that I know of. I still say the fiancé and the bridal party are the most likely ones. Sometimes the people you think you're closest to can hurt you the most."

"I say we start with the fiancé." Di circled his name. "This could have been a crime of passion."

"True. But why kill her the week before their wedding?" I doodled a scroll with leaves on the paper.

"Cold feet."

"Ha. Breaking up is easier than murder." I shook my head.

At that, my cell phone warbled, and I snatched it from the counter. *Ben!*

". . .checking in. . ." The sound of an engine roared in the background. "I miss you already."

"I miss you, too. So where are you?" I knew enough to guess about where he'd be, but I liked hearing his voice.

The bell over the front door clanged, and a pair of ladies entered. I smiled at them and shot Di a nod. She moved across the shop floor and greeted them.

After a moment of static, Ben answered. "About halfway to Phoenix."

Halfway to Phoenix. So I was right. "Hurry home, but be safe."

"I will. I'll call you when I stop."

"I'll be waiting."

When I hung up the phone, Di was showing the pair of women the Build-a-Basket-of-Soap offer. She also pointed out the coordinating scents in bath fizzies.

I stayed back and watched. She moved effortlessly and chatted with them as if they were old friends. I think one of them worked at the town library, but she looked a lot older than the last time I went in. Wasn't the other one a seamstress?

Di totaled their purchases, and I wrapped their products mutely.

"That's twenty-nine seventy," Di said. They promptly paid after taking a few business cards and the rest of the sample soaps from the dish on the counter.

After the door clanged behind them, Di turned and gave me one of those looks an older sister ought to give her younger one, not the other way around.

"What?" I took up the list we'd been working on.

"Don't 'what' me." She tapped the paper. "Something's eating at you, deeper than the store and what happened to Charla."

I only grinned at her. "You were good out there. If only I could hire you to sell."

Di waved me off. "You can sell this stuff without any help from me. But you're hanging back like it's your first day of school."

"I don't know. . . ."

"Chicken." She stuck out her tongue.

My shoulders slumped. No arguing with that. In business, in life, in love. Chicken. My eyes burned. Ben was right, and so was Di.

"I think Ben's going to propose."

Di shrieked and had me wrapped in a hug before I

knew what was happening. "What? You didn't tell me until now? Greenburg's longest-running steady couple is taking the plunge?" She stepped back and grinned.

"He hasn't asked, but he bought old Mrs. Flanders's property out near the river. Said something about it being time to settle down." The vise around my neck tightened another notch. "The idea of seeing him every day for the rest of my life. . . I'm afraid."

"I wish you'd gotten married years ago. Older people get so set in their ways."

"So I'm 'older' now, huh?" Funny how she pulled that older-sister card when she was ready to. "I'm only thirty-five."

"I didn't mean it that way. I mean that you and Ben are both on the downside of thirty, and you've both got routines you're used to. Did you think this might be scary for him, too?"

I shook my head. "I never thought about it that way." And here I'd wallowed in my own conflicted feelings the last time he was home. Ben had to be terribly brave to make such big changes in his life— buying property, building a home. I moved to brush some imaginary dust from the June Breeze and Peachy Keen displays. Although the bottom of my purse was a black hole of receipts and ballpoint pens, I arranged my soaps alphabetically in the store.

"I know Steve and I were only nineteen when we married, and we had a lot to learn about each other." Di wore a faraway expression. "You think you know someone, and then they surprise you. Some things good, some not so good."

"Do you ever feel like you missed out on anything?"

"Like what?"

Finally, the dam burst, the one I'd been shoring up those nights I couldn't go to sleep—the times I wondered about Ben being the man God had for me, everything.

"I'm just so scared I'm going to wake up one day and be like everyone else, with the whole routine of work and kids and chaos and grocery shopping and leaky faucets and. . ." I waved a hand as if all those things were swooping down on me like evil birds of prey.

"Well, I like my life." Di joined me and straightened the jars of bath salts. "And it *has* turned into all those things. But boring and stifling are what someone makes out of their life. You know what I wouldn't trade? The walks with Steve, when he reminds me I'm the only woman for him. Seeing Taylor run up to give me a drawing he colored himself. The times we go tubing down the river on a lazy summer afternoon, just the four of us. Those moments cancel out the boring stuff."

"Sorry, I didn't mean to put down what you and Steve have." I took a deep breath at the sweet pang of longing that stabbed at my heart. "I want those things, too. But there's so much out there—I don't want to look back and regret it."

"And you've spent the last how many years with this back and forth with Ben? I think you two have kept

a convenient distance from each other long enough."
Di patted my hand. "So let life happen. Embrace what
God has for you and make the most of it."

"There's a lot stacked up against me right now."
I glanced around the room. "And I don't mean
soap, either. I've got to save this business. Ben said
sometimes I give up too easily. Well, I'm not going
to. Tennessee River Soaps isn't going down without
a fight. We're going to make an appointment with
Charla's fiancé and do a little digging and see what
comes up."

"What about Mike Chandler? Didn't you want to
talk to him?"

"I do," I admitted, "but I thought maybe Charla's
fiancé might shed a little light on that lawsuit. I know, I
know, there's confidentiality and all, but cases in court
are usually a matter of public record. Maybe he can
save me the red tape of going to the courthouse and
requesting a transcript of the proceedings."

"Oh, I hadn't thought of that."

"Plus, I'm chicken when it comes to talking to
Mike. Angry men scare me, and Mike Chandler is
one angry man." I didn't need to remind Di about the
time I saw Mike throw a pallet of peaches across the
farmyard last summer. Di and I had made our weekly
pilgrimage to Chandler's Farmer's Market. I'd caught
a glimpse of him by the peach groves, his face red as
he shouted at an employee. Then there were the bitter
words at Honey's.

"So, you're going to wait to go to Chandler's until

Ben gets home again?"

"That's the plan. And the longer the murderer thinks no one suspects what they did, the more relaxed they'll get." At least I hoped so.

8

The leather-covered loveseat squeaked underneath me as I crossed my legs. I'd donned a skirt and my favorite blouse on Tuesday morning, which was Robert's first available appointment. The offices of Robert Robertson, Attorney-at-Law, extended to a twelve-foot ceiling, where a fan clanked and spun way above our heads.

"Di, you didn't need to come with me." Although deep down, I was glad. I'd never dealt with a lawyer, other than having Steve's cousin Drew help me when I launched the soap business. The connection practically made Drew family in Greenburg genealogy, and we'd drawn the papers up one night after a fish fry at Di and Steve's house. In contrast, Robert's office screamed money and power. Was that what had attracted Charla to Robert? And Kaitlyn to Robert. . .and who knows who else? Even Kaitlyn hadn't seemed impervious to Robert's charms, and that was six months into another relationship.

"I didn't mind tagging along. You can do the talking, and I'll watch him answer. Then we can compare notes." Di seemed more excited than someone ought to be in such a place. Soft music played somewhere, the sound of classical violins. It made me want to curl up on the squeaky leather and go to sleep.

The door opened to Robert's inner sanctum. "Mr.

Robertson is ready to see you now, ladies." His receptionist greeted us with a flat voice.

I had told the receptionist I needed to speak with Robert about a legal matter concerning the store. This secured me a prompt appointment without my lying to the man.

Di's eyes grew round as marbles, and I choked on my breath when we entered Robert's office. We shook hands with him, and I tried not to stare too hard. Robert gestured to a pair of wing-back chairs facing his mahogany desk. I settled onto the leather chair, which groaned as if in response to Robert's appearance.

I should explain. Greenburg is not completely a hick town. We have a few urban touches, even on the Tennessee River. A few men like Robert get manicures (though they probably drive to Jackson to get one) and possibly wear pink shirts when they get a wild hair. But these men do not wear makeup of any kind. And today Robert wore it badly.

The area under Robert's left eye had been carefully covered with some kind of concealer, but I didn't miss the hemorrhage from a ruptured blood vessel in his eye. A bruise still glowed from under the flesh-colored cover-up on his left cheek. The effect wasn't toned down any by his neutral suit and coiffed hair. I wanted to turn the ceiling fan up a notch to see if his hair moved at all.

Daddy would have said a real man doesn't try to hide his wounds. But to Robert, image was probably everything.

"So, Ms. Clark, how may I help you today?" The

words rolled off his tongue like honey. Aside from the black eye, I could see how Charla fell for his polished Southern charm. Just a year or so past thirty, with the promise of aging well with a great head of hair. The man could have been an A-list actor on the big screen. I've heard that practicing law is a form of acting, so I supposed a man like Robert enjoyed being a star on the small stage that was our county. I felt Di press the tip of her shoe onto my toes peeking out the front of my sandal. It dawned on me that I was staring. This jogged my brain back to the purpose of our visit.

"First, I wanted to say"—I focused on his nose, which was a very fine nose—"I'm sorry about what happened to Charla. I don't know how she could have had such a reaction—she and I mixed that scrub together. . . ." *Great, Andi.* Rub salt in the wound seeping from his broken heart.

"I don't blame you at all. Around here, we're attemping to continue life, life without her." He sighed and gave me a sad smile. I sensed that his thoughts were light-years away from the office. "So, what exactly is the purpose of your visit?"

"Well, I needed to ask you about my business. I'm wondering if there might be ramifications to the accident with. . .with Charla."

"Legally?" His eyebrows rose, making his black eye more prominent.

"Yes. I have insurance on my inventory, as well as liability insurance to cover accidents, if someone slips or falls, for example. But I don't own my building. I rent. Would my landlord be subject to any litigation?" I felt Di's gaze on me as I spoke. A drizzle of sweat snaked down my spine. If Robert ever ran for office, the ladies would swoon.

"That's hard to say, really. Anyone can file a lawsuit nowadays." His drawl wasn't fooling me, though. He seemed like he didn't really want to talk. Right then I realized that if I really wanted answers for these questions, I could have chosen another lawyer. Robert probably realized the same thing. Might as well go for broke, since my pretense for coming just crumbled.

I glanced at Di and leaned forward. "What would you say if I thought someone tampered with the scrub for Charla's party? My store was broken into that morning, and cash was stolen from the drawer. I think that could have been a cover for someone putting strawberry in the scrub, knowing it would give Charla a fatal allergic reaction. Can you think of someone who would do something like that?"

A gurgling noise came from Di's throat.

I shot her a soft glare.

"Ms. Clark, I probably knew Charla better than anyone." Robert paused, his gaze flicking downward to the right. I tried to remember what I'd heard once about body language. "She might have been flighty in high school and college, but like all of us, she was desperate to be loved. And I loved her. I also respected her. Men often pressure women to compromise. . .themselves. But I didn't pressure her. Throughout her life, I'm sure her beauty and charm made a lot of people jealous."

This was not new information to me. Momma had definitely been right about Charla being misunderstood, if what Robert said was true.

"I know that, Mr. Robertson. But can you think of anyone specifically who might have hated her enough to kill her? Someone who went to an awful lot of trouble?"

He looked at his desk as if he'd rather tend to the papers scattered across its surface.

"There was a former boyfriend," Robert finally said. "When Charla broke up with him, he really scared her."

"Who?" The muscles in my back twinged I'd sat so far forward in the chair.

"I'm not at liberty to say." His features closed up.

I pounced on my chance. "What about Mike Chandler? I heard she sued him last year for allegedly trying to poison her."

"Oh, that." He waved my question off as if he were brushing a fly from his beloved desk papers. "It's true, she did sue him. And yes, he was the man she was afraid of."

"Did this case actually go to trial?"

Robert made a series of rapid-fire blinks. "Last September. The judge dismissed the suit as frivolous and hearsay."

"I wonder if Mike could have nursed a grudge all this time." I ignored Di's sharp glance. "If you could tell me, please, how did Mike allegedly try to poison Charla?"

Robert gave another slow sigh. His secretary had

said the first consultation was free when I scheduled the appointment, but still I hoped he didn't have the inclination to start charging me by the hour.

"I don't see what relevance her lawsuit against Mr. Chandler has to her death." Now Robert looked bored.

"I'm not saying there is a direct connection; I'm just trying to get some questions answered. If you'd just tell me, I wouldn't have to track the information down through the courts. Or the newspaper." I wasn't sure about the newspaper angle, but I figured a Thacker would make sure they were in the news.

"All right. Charla came to my office in tears last summer after she'd been released from the hospital. She'd had a severe allergic reaction. She said Mike did it after she threatened to break up with him."

"So how did he supposedly try to poison her?"

"With strawberries, of course." Robert's eyes shone bright. "We took out a restraining order against Mike. I couldn't help falling for Charla. One thing led to another, and we were together ever since."

I made what I hoped sounded like a sympathetic noise. Yes, we would definitely check out Mike's story. But I decided to try another angle when Robert started shuffling papers as if we weren't there.

"Well, thanks for your time. I appreciate your help and advice." I scrambled to my feet. "By the way, Mr. Robertson, where were you last Saturday morning?"

He stood and placed both hands on the desk. "My best man, groomsmen, and I were at the River

Valley Country Club playing golf. You can verify this if you want to. We played golf from seven until I got the call. . . ." A wave of grief rippled over his face.

"Where'd you get that shiner?" I made no effort to disguise my stare. Someone had decked Robert but good.

"I fell in the shower."

"And where were you the night before Charla's party?"

"You know, none of this is really any of your business." He shook his head and gestured to the door. "Have a nice day."

When Di and I stepped to the front office, I glanced back over my shoulder toward Robert's open door. He was scoping us out as if we were walking the beach. Then he winked at me.

Di waved her arms in the parking lot. "He's covering up something. I just know it!"

"I almost want to apologize. I was pretty nosy there at the end." I moved to whirl around and head back inside the building, but Di caught my arm.

"Oh no, you don't. He didn't want us there, his answers to your legal questions were vague, and I can hardly blame him for being irritated, even if I don't believe him."

"Di, he was checking us out when we left, too. Some grieving fiancé—ugh!" I rubbed my arms. "Part of me feels like going back and letting him know what

I think about that."

We didn't speak as we roared down the road in my Jeep and back to the bank, where Di was due at work. She hopped out once I pulled up to the curb.

"You should call Jerry," Di suggested as she grabbed her purse from the floor of the Jeep. "I wonder if Robert's black eye has a better explanation than falling in the shower."

"I thought of that. In fact, I'll head right to the station and see if Jerry can tell me anything."

"Well, call me and tell me what you find out."

I grinned and waved, leaving Di standing on the curb.

Greenburg PD was its usual hive of small-town activity, which meant Jerry was on the phone, another officer was filling out a small mountain of forms, and Anna, the clerk, was corralling clusters of people into the waiting area. The fax machine spit out paper, its sound covered by murmuring voices.

"Morning, Andi." Anna motioned a young couple to a bench by the counter. "Here to see Jerry?"

"Yeah, just for a minute." I could see him behind the glass that separated his office from the main part of the station. He caught my eye, waved, and shifted his concentration back to the phone.

"Go ahead. You're practically family anyway." She refocused her attention on the others in the room.

I rounded the corner to Jerry's office in time to hear, "And that's all I have to say about the matter. Have a nice day." Jerry hung up the phone with a clatter. He glanced at me as I entered. "You didn't happen to bring anything from Higher Grounds, did you?"

"Nah, I skipped a trip this morning. Had an appointment." I shook my head when Jerry gestured to the chair at the desk. "I won't be long. I just have a couple of questions."

"Go ahead. I have a few minutes. Maybe ninety seconds, but I need a breather." He sat down on his wooden chair, which complained with a *squeal*.

"Have you heard anything from the lab?"

"About. . . ?"

"My scrub, Jer."

"No, it's still waiting its turn.

"Well, I discovered something interesting in my main container of scrub. Strawberry seeds. I think someone found a way to get strawberry into the cherry scrub. Someone who knew Charla was allergic."

"At the very least, that would be a mean prank."

"At the very most, it would be murder, or perhaps involuntary manslaughter since she died, even if whoever did this hadn't meant to kill her." The realization dawned on me. What if whoever did this had only meant it as a cruel prank that backfired?

"I see what you're getting at. But what motive? Charla seemed to be well liked—on some levels." Jerry seemed ready for me to go.

Silence hovered between us.

"Andi, I don't have a lot of time this morning. Everyone's here complaining about a well-intentioned rookie in the next office, and I've got some fires to put out, so to speak. I think your theory is interesting, but until we have concrete evidence—"

"I'll bring the scrub in and show you if I have to."

"It doesn't prove anything. There's no case. I need more than some seeds in some soap flakes."

I tried not to bristle. "Do you know much about Mike Chandler? He was an ex-boyfriend of Charla's with a bad temper. And Robert, her fiancé, is sporting a rather large black eye this morning."

Jerry sat up straight and stared at me. "Matter of fact, I do. Mike was just released from the lockup this morning."

9

I changed my mind about not sitting down and took the seat across from Jerry's desk. "Why?"

"We got a call to Robert Robertson's office last evening. Turns out Mike showed up and got into an altercation with him."

"I saw that someone had landed quite a punch." My heart pounded in my chest. "And Robert wouldn't talk about what happened."

"Same here." Jerry tilted back in his chair. "In fact, he wouldn't press charges for assault. We only had enough to slap Chandler with disturbing the peace."

"It's got to be about Charla."

"When Tim got there last night, Mike had already worn off his rage. Came along pretty quietly." Jerry shrugged. "In fact, he's probably the only person not complaining about Tim this morning."

I stood before I started mulling over the idea of Mike slugging Robert because of Charla. It didn't add up, but then crimes of passion usually didn't. On one hand, Mike would have wanted to watch her suffer, but on the other hand, attacking Robert? The pieces had to fit somehow, but I had the feeling I still lacked a few from this puzzle.

"Thanks, Jerry. You've been a big help. Next time I'll bring you a tall, double-shot latte."

"I'll hold you to that. Glad I could help *somebody*

today." He stood, relieving the poor desk chair, which groaned again. "Say hi to Ben next time he calls. And tell him that contractor gave him an estimate." I nodded then left the station.

Ben liked his routines and was a big boy, capable of making his own decisions. But I thought we'd been together long enough that we'd share major decisions with each other. When I decided to start the soap business, Ben had helped me every step of the way. His good sense kept me from going in ten different directions. I figured he would include me, as well. But a contractor? An estimate? He said he wasn't in a hurry, if I remembered right. He'd have some 'splaining to do once he got home, and I'd ask him in the nicest possible way. Although I wasn't sure what he needed to explain.

I thought back to the interview with Robert and continued pondering the hunch that had come over me in his office. I had felt his grief, noticed the redness in his eyes that wasn't from getting punched. I'd noted the fine lines of weariness, too, that signaled lack of sleep. He'd loved Charla and lost her, and he appeared to be trying to piece together life without her.

Yet, I reminded myself, he was an actor of sorts. What if Robert had been trying to throw me off about Mike? Robert knew the details of Charla's lawsuit against Mike. Although Mike had been cleared, I wondered if pointing a finger at Mike would be a way for Robert to cover his own tracks.

Ridiculous. I started the Jeep and headed for the

store. The man had been a week away from marrying Charla. What possible reason could he have for breaking it off, let alone trying to kill her right before the wedding? At this point, I couldn't venture to guess why.

—

I sat at my desk at the store and watched my e-mail in-box fill up with Internet orders from the Tennessee River Soaps Web site. I allowed myself to smile at this bright spot. No one in Bangor, Austin, or Ocean City cared that someone had keeled over amid the soaps in my shop. The deposits to my account would help bridge the gap in slow sales at the store.

No, I had not forgotten about Mike Chandler and the black eye. Most sleuths have to earn a living. I knew I did. I couldn't run around chasing leads with a business to run. Which is why, since talking to Jerry, I'd spent a few days going through inventory, brainstorming promotions, and shoring up the crumbling foundation of my business. That, and waiting for Ben to come home.

"Miss Clark?" Sadie appeared in the doorway between my office alcove and the front of the store. "I finished those displays for you."

"Thanks." I stood and stretched. "Let me take a look at them." Sadie, the thoughtful teen from my Sunday school class, had volunteered to give me a hand at the store. We'd already brainstormed a few print ads for the newspaper.

We walked into the sales area together. She'd arranged

the soaps by floral, fruit, and miscellaneous scents. She'd used some seashells and sand to make a summer tabletop display.

"This is super." I smiled at the teenager, and she glowed. "Did you say you were going to college for design?"

She nodded. "I start at Vanderbilt this fall. Interior design." The briefest hint of a shadow crossed her face.

"What's wrong?"

"It's Kyle."

"Kyle?" I couldn't remember him from Sunday school class, although I did recall one young man looking at Sadie with puppy-dog eyes while they talked in the hall at church.

"I—I don't want to leave him."

"What's he planning to do?"

"He said he's going to stay here and work, but I was hoping he'd put in a transfer and come to Nashville to work. We could still see each other while I'm in school, and I know he could make it in the music business. Miss Clark, he's so talented. He writes songs and plays the guitar and sings. . . ." Sadie's voice trailed off. "But at the same time. . ."

"Yes?"

"We're so young, and I'd hate for him to come out there just for me and get disappointed. You and Mr. Hartley have a long-distance relationship, with him being on the road so much, don't you?"

I wanted to say, "Yes, and Ben and I are twice your age," only I didn't.

"And you've made it work, right?" She swirled the sand in the Summer Fun display with her finger.

"Now that's the ten-thousand-dollar question, isn't it?" I wasn't sure how to answer her question. I didn't want to raise her hopes and tell her, yes, they could make it work, too. "Ben and I have been together seven years. We've had our ups and downs, but we pray a lot. We make each other a priority even when we're apart."

"So are you going to get married?" Her voice held a teasing tone.

"I suppose we will." I moved to the flower garden display, where Sadie had arranged silk ferns and greenery around the soap shelves.

"What's taken you so long? I don't think Kyle and I could wait *that* long. . . . I mean. . ." When she paused, I glanced her way. Her cheeks were shot with red.

"I—I really can't say." My stomach quavered at Sadie's pointed questions. The way young people got to the heart of matters blew me away. No being vague and noncommittal like some of us older folks.

"Well, I say if you find the love of your life and you know he's the one God has for you, why wait to get married?" Sadie smiled.

I had to smile at her frank simplicity. "Sadie, you and Kyle should talk and pray together about your future. You're so young and still trying to find the path God has for you. I don't feel like I'm the best person to offer you advice in matters of the heart. But I can say this: You're right. It's not easy having a long-distance relationship. You two should communicate about this, especially before you leave."

She gave me a hug. "Oh, Miss Clark, you're so smart. You've helped me so much."

"You've been a big help to me today, too. This place has had quite a face-lift."

Sadie picked up her purse from behind the counter. "I'll help anytime you need me. But I've got to go help my mom with Nana now."

"That's fine. I'll see you on Sunday." I waved as she breezed through the front door and went to her car. *To be eighteen again.* Would I have done things differently?

I felt a smidge hypocritical as I walked back to my office. I was a fine one to talk to Sadie about communicating with her boyfriend. Lately it felt as if Ben and I had fallen short in that area.

Ben was home, though, and had dropped large hints about me making some strawberry shortcake. A visit to Chandler's Farmer's Market was at the top of my to-do list. Ben planned to stop by the store after Sadie and I finished our work.

Two birds would die today, felled by the single stone. I would take Ben to get some strawberries, and we could talk to Mike together. The matter of finding out who killed Charla Thacker still weighed on me, and Ben was the best backup I could think of without dragging anyone else into the matter. I didn't want to bring Daddy with me and have him ask me a hundred questions.

I zinged through the orders until two, when I

heard Ben's truck horn outside the store. After I shut down the computer, I jerked a brush through my hair.

Ben called through the back door, "You ready?"

"Be right there!" I grabbed my bag and hurried to lock the store.

We soon left Greenburg city limits behind and roared down the road to the farmer's market. My heart sang when Ben raised my hand and kissed it.

"We'll have four whole days together," I said. "When I'm not at the store, of course." Fear of the future slithered back to where I'd held it at bay.

"How's the store doing, by the way?"

"Holding its own for now. I have a whole slew of Internet orders to box and ship, which is great."

Ben's smile warmed me. "I'm proud of you, seeing this through. I really am."

"Thanks. That means a lot." My earlier conversation with Sadie rang in my ears. "Sadie from church gave me a hand. She's a sweet girl and has a real eye for design."

"That must be the girl my aunt's stepbrother's grandson, Kyle, is dating."

It figures. Everyone's related somehow in Greenburg, at least by marriage. "Huh?"

"Aunt Bette's stepbrother has a grandson named Kyle. Can play a mean guitar." Ben turned onto Hillside cutoff, across the river west of town, on the road to Shiloh.

"That's the one. Sadie was talking to me about long-distance relationships. She's going away this fall. Sounds like Kyle's planning to stay here."

"What'd you tell her?"

"That long-distance relationships are work, and couples really need to pray together and communicate."

"Good advice."

"I thought so."

We fell silent. I had nothing more to add, unless you counted the fact that I thought Ben and I needed to communicate more.

I broke our silence first. "I have a confession to make. I have an ulterior motive today besides buying strawberries."

"How's that?"

"I'm going to talk to Mike Chandler about his lawsuit against Charla Thacker last year. After what we heard at Honey's the last time you were home, I wonder if he might have had something to do with sabotaging my cherry scrub."

Ben didn't reply, and I glanced his way. His focus remained fixed on the road, his forehead creased in thought.

"You know, I've got a confession to make, too." Ben sighed. "Only it's not the one I planned on making."

"What are you talking about?"

"I could have killed somebody once."

"What?" I gaped at him.

"A guy named Nate. I could have killed him back in high school."

"Ben—"

"Really. He cheated off my test, and then when I reported him, he said I gave him the answers. We both failed. I was off the baseball team that year because of failing that class. I dreamed of punching him until I couldn't punch him anymore. I can still imagine his bloody nose, his black eyes. Missing teeth."

I sucked in a deep breath. "But you didn't—"

"I wanted to. One day after school. To take one swing. Only one. The thought of letting go like that scared me." His voice sounded raspy, and he cleared his throat. "Then someone did jump him, put him in the hospital for a week. That could've been me."

"I never knew. . ." Seven years we'd been a couple. Seven years, and I'd never seen him hit anything except a baseball. Steve had dragged him to play golf once, and rumor had it Ben had wanted to hit a tree with his driver.

"You know what else scared me? Part of me realized how much I wanted to hurt him." He ran his fingers through my hair that blew back in the breeze from the open window. That such gentle hands could have been capable of violence was unthinkable. "Deep down, but for the grace of God, I could have been a murderer."

"It's not the same." I felt like I was floundering. But it wasn't the same, was it?

"Do you really know for sure?" Ben moved his hand back to the wheel. "Maybe Mike's got a hot head, but that doesn't mean anything."

"I plan on finding out." I swallowed hard then faced the window and let the warm, humid breeze flow over me. It spoke of life and growth, not rage and senseless vengeance.

The market came into view. Cars filled the muddy parking lot in front of a large, covered open-air pavilion that looked like a red and black barn without the walls. I caught glimpses of brightly colored produce displayed on tables and glass jars that glowed amber in the sunshine. Ben aimed the truck for an empty gap between two cars.

"I didn't bring my mud boots." I stuck my head out the window and looked at the ground. Leftover rainwater mingled with the grass and red mud a couple of inches deep.

"No problem." Ben left the truck and came around the hood to stand at my door. "Piggyback." He opened the door with a *squeal* of hinges.

"You've got to be kidding. I'll break your back." I wasn't overly round, but then I wasn't like one of those toothpick women who can fit into children's clothes, either.

"Seriously." He turned his back to me. "C'mon."

I put my feet on the truck's running board and slung my bag over my shoulder. "I can't believe we're doing this." He caught my legs as I wrapped my arms around his shoulders, and he started to walk.

We moved forward to a dry patch of grass, and Ben made little strangling noises. "Very funny," I said.

"I'm not joking," he gasped.

I loosened my grip on his neck. Evidently one of my arms had slid up to his throat. "Sorry about that."

"Ands, you've got to trust me. I won't let you fall." He stopped when we reached a damp patch of grass, and my feet slipped to the ground. Ben frowned before he took my hand.

"I do trust you."

"More than carrying you piggyback?"

"Of course I do." I grinned at him. "I just didn't want to fall into the mud."

He looked as if he didn't believe me.

"What's wrong?" I knew better than to try to drag an explanation out of him, but first with him buying Doris Flanders's property, and then what Jerry said about a house estimate. . .

"I—I need to show you something, but later. Now's not the time." His brief hint of a smile told me he wasn't mad, but his behavior puzzled me.

"All right, later then. Let's get the strawberries." This was not how I had envisioned the afternoon. I'd pictured us holding hands, catching up on time spent apart. Sidestepping puddles. Trading stories and laughing. That and coaxing information out of Mike with Ben's help. Instead, I asked questions and received one-syllable answers. I trusted Ben. I just didn't want to be dropped. What was the big deal?

Silence hung between us as we wove between the vehicles and approached the pavilion. I had no idea what I'd said or done and stifled several questions before they slipped out. All I knew was that I had started eating those words I'd spoken to Sadie. But you couldn't very well communicate with someone who didn't want to talk. Ben did say we'd talk later, so I tried to content myself with that knowledge. We rounded the puddles, and my sneakers ended up getting muddy anyway.

"Ben, did I do something?" The words slipped out before I could stop them.

"No, it's me this time." He paused at a table of round, plump tomatoes, half of them ripe and red, the other half green.

"These look good. I think I'll get some." I chose a basket of each and paid for them. "What can I do to help you?"

"Just be here." Ben took one of the baskets from me. "Because. . .sometimes you confuse me. With one breath you sound thrilled to see me, and with the next breath you sound like you're trying to push me away."

"I'm sorry. I don't mean to come across like that." My mouth watered at the thought of fried green tomatoes. *Comfort food, here I come.*

"What have we been doing all these years?" Ben took the other basket from me. "Why didn't I ask you to marry me sooner?"

Where was this coming from? Here I'd been planning to coach Ben on what to look for when I talked to Mike. Not this. "I don't know, Ben." I couldn't admit that the thought of getting married both thrilled and terrified me at the same time.

"The years have flown by, haven't they?"

Now he sounded like he was at the brink of a midlife crisis a few years early.

"Sometimes I wish you could come home from the road, but I don't know what you'd do for work." The idea hit me like a wave. He had hit the road after his uncle's construction company folded and hadn't looked back. He hadn't asked me if I minded him going out on the road, either, but at that time we hadn't been a couple for long. Now I was thirty-five, and he was thirty-seven. Time hadn't stopped for us.

"What if I did come home? Where would we be, then?"

My throat caught, and I opened my mouth to answer.

"Ben Hartley, how's it going?" Someone from the church softball team clapped Ben on the back. They chatted for a few minutes as I scanned the area. I thought I saw a man with a goatee at the far corner. Mike. My pulse pounded. Just thinking about talking to him was like planning to give a bath to a Rottweiler.

"You ready to get those strawberries?" Ben turned back to me and touched my arm.

I nodded, and we headed for the corner where I thought I'd seen Mike standing behind a table full of red strawberries. He was stacking a fresh tray of green plastic baskets that brimmed with the red fruit. His right hand was wrapped in a bandage.

"Hi there, Mr. Chandler."

A glimmer of a smile flashed across Mike's face. "Call me Mike. Mr. Chandler's my daddy."

So far, so good. "Andi Clark. I, um, run the soap store in town."

He gave us each a glance. "Ah, so that's your place?"

"That's right." I pointed to some of the strawberries.

"I need a few of those."

"Good deal. I'll probably have a couple more weeks of berries; then that's it for the year." He shrugged. "Should have a ton of watermelons, though, so stop back. Fourth of July's not far off."

"No, it's not." I looked at Ben, hoping he'd say something. Make some guy small talk. Anything. Fishing? I already knew how much he hated golf.

"So, how's business?" Mike asked.

"It could be better," I admitted. "All new businesses struggle at first, but I'm hoping things will pick up after this recent setback."

"Yep, Charla Thacker's been a setback to a lot of people." Mike's jaw tightened.

"*She* wasn't responsible for what happened." Since Ben was choosing to stay mum at the moment, I took matters into my own hands. "But I'm wondering if someone else was."

"I call it poetic justice." At his harsh tone, several passersby glanced at us and continued on their way.

"You seem pretty angry at her."

"And her creep of a fiancé."

"I saw his face." I decided to strike with my knowledge. "So why'd you hit him?"

Mike frowned. "Some people don't deserve what they get. He didn't. Not with all his money. He didn't deserve her."

I rubbed my forehead. "Mike, I don't understand. She sued you for trying to poison her with strawberries last summer. I heard you say you would've liked to have seen her suffer. Yet you went and decked her fiancé."

Mike's eyes flashed. "He's slime. I never would have done to Charla what he did. I might have a short fuse that burns fast, but I'm not a lying, two-faced cheat."

"What did he do?" Maybe I was on to something about Robert not seeming as grief-stricken as he appeared.

"You know what? It's not for me to say." Mike blinked and stared at the baskets of strawberries.

And then I knew. "You still loved her, didn't you?"

"They say you always hurt the one you love." Mike's brow furrowed. "She and I, we did. Maybe I did some stupid stunts, and maybe she was shallow, but I loved her."

"What about killing someone?"

Mike placed both hands on the table and looked me straight in the eye. "Yeah, at one time I probably could've killed her."

After that lawsuit, I wanted her to suffer for almost putting me out of business. I had to take out a loan to float me through the rest of last summer, and I'll be paying on that for another couple years. By that time she'll be worm food. Ironic."

The sounds of the market faded to nothing, and my pulse roared in my ears. My throat burned. While this information was nothing new, hearing him and seeing him say the words to my face was downright terrifying.

I felt Ben's presence next to me. He slipped his arm around my waist. Despite our earlier prickly feelings, I had no doubt of his loyalty. I also understood a silent *I told you so* from him as I remembered the story he'd told me on the way over in the truck.

"So. . .how much for the strawberries?" I gestured to the tray, figuring I'd buy extra.

"On the house." Mike waved off the money I held out. "It figures I should sympathize with you about Charla."

"No, I couldn't do that. You need paying customers, too."

Mike straightened. "Before you run to the cops and claim I tried to kill her and succeeded at last, you ought to know something."

"What's that?"

"I wouldn't have gone to all that trouble of trying to set up an allergy attack. I mean, c'mon. A shotgun would've been much simpler. That's what I told 'em last year when she tried to smear my name through town right before we broke up."

A petite brunette approached from the direction of the main house and sidled up to him. Mike slid his arm around her and kissed her on the nose.

"Hey, sweetie." Mike's throat bobbed, and he shot me a look that screamed the conversation was over. "We having lunch in a while?"

"Yup, I'm driving over to Honey's for some box lunches." She smiled at us. "Hi, y'all."

"Hi." I picked up my strawberries. "You two have a great day."

Ben and I trudged from the open-air market.

"Now that was interesting." I kept replaying Mike's words in my mind. We found Ben's truck, and he popped our produce onto the seat between us.

"I'll say."

I climbed into the truck. Mike's mood puzzled me. Anger, betrayal, rage, revenge. His demeanor rang out that he still loved her, but he wanted her to suffer for dumping him, for hurting his business. Mike's rage at Robert also had me baffled. I mentally crossed him off our suspect list. . .for now.

It only made sense that he wouldn't have gone through the subterfuge of sabotage. If he was forthright enough to confront Robert physically, he'd have done the same with Charla. When he said he'd have shot her if he really wanted her dead, I believed him.

Ben fired up my charcoal grill outside while I sliced freshly washed strawberries for shortcake in my kitchen. We'd stopped at the grocery store after the farmer's market and picked up some rib eyes, which were now marinating in the fridge. Ben came inside and swiped a berry from the basket before I could slap his hand away.

"You know, while I was on the road, I listened to a late-night radio talk show about murderers and serial killers," Ben said.

"That's a creepy choice for late-night listening." I looked at him and shuddered. "And you out there on the road by yourself." It wasn't like Ben couldn't hold his own in a fight—not that he'd ever had to. His burly stance was usually enough to intimidate some people.

"Didn't bother me. But I remember an interesting comment the profiler made. About the killer's gender and MO."

Why didn't he just come out and say it? I dumped a handful of sugar over the strawberries and stirred. "And what's that?"

"Female killers tend to use poisons. It sounds like something a woman would do, spiking your scrub with strawberries." He poured us each a tall glass of tea.

I handed him the foil-wrapped bundle of salted onions and butter to place on the grill. "You think?"

"Really. What guy would go to all the trouble of messing with your face cream? I don't even know what you do with that stuff half the time." Ben set his glass of tea down on the counter. "Now a woman? A woman would pull a mean stunt like that."

"Oh, that's a low blow. So you're saying men believe in swift vengeance?" I slung a damp dish towel in Ben's direction, which he caught with one hand as he grinned. He carried the onion packet outside to the grill on the back patio, and I brought my glass of iced tea outside with me.

"Seriously." Ben lifted the lid and laid the packet on the grill. "A guy wouldn't go through the hassle of doing something he wouldn't be sure worked and that he probably wouldn't see. You said Mike mentioned he'd have liked to have seen Charla suffer. What guy would know about the party, or even care? Except for Charla's fiancé."

"You've got a point." I set my tea on the patio table and sank onto a lawn chair. Ben took the one opposite mine. "I feel so silly. I practically tried to drag a confession out of Mike. I almost feel like I should apologize to him or something."

"You want answers. No one can blame you for that. I've gotta admit it sounded crazy, but the more I think about it, you might be on to something—about her death being no accident."

"I'm glad you're on my side." My heart beat faster at the idea that Ben believed in me. After all his poohpoohing the idea of someone trying to kill Charla, this felt like a major breakthrough. I had to get some evidence, though, something to bring to Jerry, since obviously the man's hands were full.

The fact that Ben had reminded me of our wide suspect list didn't help any. A woman who hated Charla enough to kill her. Sure, the police could drag in a lineup of women with grudges due to their own broken hearts—or the suffering of sisters or friends.

"I *am* on your side." Ben stood. "Hey. I'd like to show you something. Be right back. Gotta get something out of the truck." He left the patio and rounded the corner of the house closest to the driveway.

I inhaled the aroma of onions on the grill and closed my eyes. Whatever mood Ben had been in on the way to the market, it had passed. When I heard his returning footsteps, I looked in his direction. He stepped onto the patio stones, a catalog in his hands.

"What's that?" I couldn't make out the cover other than part of a roof set against some treetops.

Ben turned the catalog so I could see the front. "Er, it's house plans."

"House plans?" But I'd heard him right and no mistake. *Handcrafted Homes* proclaimed that inside its pages were fifty floor plans—"for the home of your dreams."

He settled back onto his chair. "Yes. For the property I bought. I'm planning to get started on the house."

As the pages turned, my stomach and heart both did somersaults.

"I've spent these past years like a nomad. But I've been praying and hashing the idea over a lot lately. Ands, it's time I come home to Greenburg. For good."

I pulled the catalog across the table to give myself something to look at and to still my shaking hands. Four bedrooms, three bedrooms. A cabin with a loft.

"What do you think?" Ben touched a page that showed a three-bedroom floor plan with a kitchen large enough to toss a football in. "I really like this one. It has a big front porch."

"I like it, too." The house had two bathrooms, as well. Growing up at Momma and Daddy's made me long for more than one bathroom in the house. "The kitchen's huge."

His smile calmed my roiling stomach. "I thought you'd like that one."

I could only nod. "Jerry. . .he mentioned something to me about someone calling with a house estimate right before you got home."

"Aw, I was going to surprise you."

"Well, it worked. I'm surprised." I felt a smile work its way across my face. "You were already checking on estimates?"

"To see what kind of financing I'd need, although I'd like to pay for it as I build. I still know some good general contractors, and I can save money by doing lots of the finish work and tile myself."

Another nod from me. "This. . .this is a big change."

Ben took my hands in his. "I know. Change is part of life, you know."

"It'd be wonderful to have you home all the time. I'm sure it'll take some getting used to. . . ." The strength in his hands worked its way up my arms, and my trembling stilled. *Ben. Home. A real life with him.*

"It will." Ben smiled. "That's why I wanted to talk to you about the house first. I'm sorry Jerry said something."

"Don't worry about it." I scanned the other pages of house plans. "I just wish. . ."

"Wish what?"

"You already seem like you've decided this." My eyes burned. "I wish you would have talked to me sooner."

Ben's smile vanished. "You don't want me to come home?"

"It's not that at all. I feel. . .left out of the decision, maybe?"

"But you don't seem to know what you want sometimes, so I didn't tell you. And you seemed happy I'd bought the property."

This was the last time I would give Sadie, or anyone else, relationship advice. If anyone had messed up communication, it was Ben and me. "I'm sorry, Ben."

"And I'm sorry it seemed like I was planning all this without you." He took my hand. "Believe me, I've thought about you through this whole process."

My throat felt dry. "What will you do for work?"

"I've saved enough so I can maybe start my own business. Like you. I'm not sure, but everything will come together."

"I hope so." I forced a smile to my face. My usually safe Ben picks *now* as the time to get adventurous? He gave me a quick kiss before going to get the rib eyes from the refrigerator.

When he emerged a few minutes later, I'd managed to give myself a headache from sucking down half my glass of tea. The house with the front porch did look nice, though. Comfortable and not too flashy. Was this what I wanted?

"You're still not happy about the house?" Ben sat down after putting the rib eyes on the grill.

"Ben." I pinched between my eyebrows. "The one with the big porch is growing on me. But putting that aside. . ."

"What?"

"Have you ever been afraid you might miss out on something?" Unbidden tears that I didn't understand pricked my eyes. "My daddy, he was a dreamer. And is. His dream didn't come true. And I feel like us Clarks, well, we're nobodies. Always have been. Almost-but-not-quites."

"You know that's not true. . . ."

I shrugged. "I read in the Bible about how God looks at us. I believe it. At least, I can say I do. But I feel like I'm bigger than this town—I mean, my dreams are."

"Then why didn't you leave?"

I let Ben's question hang in the air between us as he went to check the grill, although a scant minute or so had passed since he put the steaks on.

"I don't know. Maybe I wanted to prove to them I didn't have to be like every other Clark—get married young, keep house, have babies, have no life beyond this town."

"Andromeda Clark, I love you with every fiber of my being. I don't care if you run a soap shop. If you want to move somewhere else, we can start our life there. So long as I'm with you." He moved closer and pulled me into his arms.

Ben's embrace tightened, and those traitorous tears came again. "I feel so silly, Ben. I'm sorry for frustrating you."

"Don't be afraid, Ands. God's dreams for you are bigger than you can imagine," he whispered in my ear.

Now if I could just convince myself of that.

When Ben left, the late-afternoon sun beat down on me and drove me inside the house to clean the kitchen. Instead of having trembling hands and butterflies over house plans, I felt empty. I'd tried to pray, but my words didn't make sense to me. I knew the Lord could sort out my feelings. Wouldn't it be nice if feelings came with switches that you could just flip off or change the setting when needed?

Practically speaking, I couldn't understand what Ben was thinking, leaving a high-paying job to come home to Greenburg. Don't get me wrong. A truck driver's expenses border on insane, but even driving a rig pays more than most jobs in Greenburg. Ben didn't even ask me before buying the property, which still hurt just a little. I shuddered at thoughts of the unknown.

But what about somewhere else? Maybe Ben was right. We *could* live somewhere else. The very thought was liberating. But I couldn't ask him to do that. Jerry was here, my family was here, and he'd bought that property.

Then I stopped scrubbing an already gleaming plate in the soapy water. The verse about perfect love casting out fear came to my mind. I cringed as I recalled the last part of the verse, about whoever fears not being made perfect in love, because fear involves torment.

For the first time, I understood what could make Charla walk away from a guy. Maybe the girl had cold feet. I ought to have my head examined. Wasn't this what I really wanted, deep down, despite my fears? Seeing Ben more often and building a real life with him?

Di would make a great set of ears. I gave up on washing the dishes and tried her house number then her cell phone.

"Hey, what's going on? The boys and I are leaving the pool. You should have come." I could hear the roar of the car's engine and my nephews' chatter in the background. "I know, but Ben and I went to Chandler's for some strawberries."

"So what did you find out? Is Mike the one?"

"I don't think Mike is our guy. From what Ben said and how Mike acted, I think Charla's murderer was most likely a woman."

"I was afraid of that." Her voice changed. "Taylor—sit yourself down on the seat and get that buckle fastened—*don't you make me pull over!*"

I jerked the phone from my ear.

"Sorry, Andi," came her voice from the phone in my hand.

I settled the phone back to my ear. "No problem. Glad I'm on your good side. And I always wear my seat belt."

"Just wait 'til you have kids."

"Ha-ha. Can you do me a favor? Keep your ears open at the bank for anything about Charla."

"Oh, the hotbed of town gossip. Yuck. I already told you I'm not good at finding clues. I sleuth vicariously through you."

"You'll know a clue when you hear it. Anything about Charla, Robert, or any of those people we've talked about. If I've got to weed through a patch of vengeful, jealous women to get to the truth, so be it. Of course I don't want to stir up any rumors, but like I said, keep your ears open."

"I still think Robert the fiancé was up to something," Di said. "Why would Mike punch him and Robert not press charges? That doesn't sound very lawyerish to me."

"That's true." I rubbed my aching temples. A stress headache had begun its twisting journey across the tops of my eyebrows. "I feel like we're looking at a bunch of little signs that add up to one big billboard of an answer, and I can't figure out what it is."

"Well, sleep on it, then." Di's voice sounded warm, almost like Momma's. "Let's talk about happier subjects. Like you and Ben. That's getting better, isn't it?"

"Ha." I shrugged, even though she couldn't see me. "He's showing me house plans."

Di's squeal pierced my ears far worse than her stern momma bellow did. "Wow, that's great!"

"Yes, and I dissolved into a puddle of tears. First I was a little upset, maybe still am, because Ben didn't ask me. He makes all these decisions and doesn't ask me until he's already put plans in motion." Now I sounded like a spoiled child.

"Hon, it's not as if you acted like you wanted him to come home."

"I know, but—"

"You're scared again."

"I am." The dishes had to be dry by now. I moved to the drainer to put the plates away. "I don't like change. But I'm working on it."

"So says the woman who's had four businesses in the last five years."

"Well, I don't. I also like to succeed. Just call me an underachieving overachiever."

"You firstborn are so driven."

"I love Ben, I really do."

"Then pray—and relax. Either you believe God can direct your steps, or you don't."

"Ouch." I glared at the phone and put it back to my ear.

"It's true."

"You're right. You are. You're telling me everything I've been trying to tell myself; only I've had a hard time listening."

"That's your problem right there. Talking to yourself."

I sighed. "Promise me you'll listen at the bank?"

"I will." Di paused. "We just pulled up to the Burger Barn. Talk to you later?"

"Sure. Thanks, Di." I disconnected the call and placed the phone handset on the table. A murderer lurked in Greenburg, or so I believed. Someone who thought they'd gotten away with their deed. But they wouldn't. Not with Di keeping her ears open, and not with me chipping away to find the truth.

The next day, I had a bit of sunshine enter when Sadie brought her grandmother to Tennessee River Soaps.

"No, Nana, this isn't the candle store at the mall; it's Miss Clark's store in town." Sadie held her grandmother's arm as the elderly woman took in the sight of the salesroom. Ever since Charla's death, Sadie had kept up her crusade to save the store by visiting twice a week and buying something, even if it was only a bar of soap. I couldn't imagine how many bath fizzies the girl had stockpiled at home.

"Hi there. How are y'all doing this morning?" I moved from behind the counter.

"We're doing great, Miss Clark." Sadie beamed. "Nana wanted to go out today, so I thought this would be as good a place as any to bring her."

"Everything smells so pretty." Sadie's nana ran her fingers across the wrapped glycerin soaps. "These look like flowers."

"That they do." At least someone appreciated the soap with its brightly colored insets that formed a daisy. "I hope they smell as good as real daisies."

"Miss Clark, you're still planning on chaperoning the youth group picnic this weekend, aren't you?" Sadie held a packet of bath salts up to her nose and inhaled. "I love this one."

"Yes, I'm planning to be there. Ben will be, too." My heart both leaped and shuddered at the thought. He was out on a short trip this time but would be back again in time to come with me to the picnic.

Sadie had quickly become one of my favorite students in the high school Sunday school class. Students like her made up for the ones who broke my heart, the ones who desperately needed to learn how to have a close relationship with God but pushed both Him and me away. Those were the ones I'd tried to reach out to so far this summer. Take Charla's cousin Seth Mitchell, who'd managed to come the weekend before. Hopefully the upcoming picnic would encourage others to come. Like him.

"So where did it happen?" Nana's sharp gaze darted around the room.

"Did what happen?" The words came out, even though I realized what Nana had meant. My heart sank.

"That poor girl. Charla Rae." Nana shook her head.

"Nana, I thought we agreed not to talk about that." Sadie laid a hand on her grandmother's arm. "We're trying to *help* Miss Clark."

"I changed my mind." Nana straightened her shoulders and picked up one of the baskets customers used to carry their purchases in while they shopped. "I'm eighty-nine, and at my age I oughtta have the right to change my mind."

Sadie looked at me and shrugged.

"Don't worry, Sadie." Now my smile felt pasted on. "Yes, ma'am, Charla Rae passed away in this very room, and I think it was a terrible tragedy."

Nana took my arm with her free hand. "Right here, you say? What a shame. She and her sister, Melinda, were my best students."

"Oh, they took piano lessons from you?" I led Nana to the other counter, which had a sink. "Here, you can try a soap sample if you'd like."

Her dark eyes snapped with humor. "So, you got any soapy surprises for me today, young lady?"

"Um, what do you mean?"

"I won't be in any danger, will I?" Nana turned on the water then started unwrapping a sample of Rambling Rose hand soap.

"Nana!" Sadie's voice squeaked across the room. I nodded to her over my shoulder, trying to reassure her everything was fine.

This was the last thing I needed. Just when it seemed like sales were starting to look up a little. A customer wondering if she'd keel over if she tried my products. And saying it to my face. The joke stung a little.

"Oh no, I think you should be fine." I cleared my throat. "Charla had an unfortunate allergic reaction. You're not allergic to anything, are you?" Nana stuck her hands under the water then started lathering her hands with the soap. "Smells lovely. No, not allergic. I think that allergy stuff is a bunch of nonsense anyway."

"You do?"

"I think some people *want* to be allergic. If they would just make up their minds not to be allergic, they wouldn't be." Nana, apparently pleased with the soap, finished rinsing her hands and turned off the water. "Got a towel, sugar?"

I mutely handed her a paper towel from the stack by the sink. For some reason, I didn't think informing Nana about the effect of histamines in the body as an involuntary reaction would convince her.

"Thank you kindly." She dried her hands and threw the paper towel on the floor just as a cell phone's ring filled the store.

Sadie pulled a phone from her purse and blushed. "Y'all go ahead and visit." She answered the call and was soon deep in conversation.

Nana shook her head. "Young people. All these gadgets don't seem to do us a bit of good. Couldn't help Charla Rae, either."

I nodded. "Did you know her well? You said she was a student of yours?"

"Both she and Melinda were." Nana paused and looked toward the front window, but I had the suspicion she wasn't seeing the sunny summer day outside. "Came to me every week for ten years, the both of them. Started when they were five and seven. Like clockwork."

"That's a long time."

"Helped pay for my groceries many a time, and I'm grateful to God for them. For all my students." Nana trudged to the summer soap display and started pushing the seashells around in the sand.

"Did you have many students?" I'd always wanted lessons, but growing up we didn't have much money to spare.

"Oh, always four or five every week. Some would come, some would go." Nana beamed. "One played at Carnegie Hall eventually. I was so proud."

"Who played better?" Hopefully Nana would redirect her focus to the Thacker sisters.

"What do you mean?"

"The Thackers—Melinda and Charla."

"Oh, Melinda did, and that sure got Charla Rae's goat." Nana chuckled and turned back to face me. "Charla always wanted to have the spotlight, and this time Melinda had her in the shadow."

My pulse quickened. "Did Melinda seem like she was in Charla's shadow otherwise?"

"Everyone lives in someone else's shadow." Nana frowned at the basket in her hands then glanced at Sadie, who was closing her cell phone. "Freda, are you about ready?"

A sympathetic smile crossed Sadie's face. "Nana, I'm Sadie. Freda's my momma." She looked at me and raised her eyebrows. "Nana gets confused."

Nana stomped over to the register and slammed her basket on the counter so hard the bars of soap inside jumped. "I'm not confused. I know exactly where I am. Freda, it ain't funny to talk about me like I'm not here."

Then Nana turned and glanced out the front window. "What happened? I told you I wanted to go to the mall today."

"You're mistaken," Sadie replied. "We went to lunch, and you said you wanted to see where Charla Thacker died." *Sorry*, she mouthed at me.

"No problem, ladies." My heart panged for Sadie and her grandmother. I moved to the register and took the soaps from Nana's basket. "Is this all you wanted to buy today?"

"I don't know." Nana shook her head. "Freda, why would I buy all this soap when I've got a package of Ivory at home I ain't even used yet?" She took a step back and made a pushing motion with her hands, as if the soap were threatening her somehow.

Sadie's expression grew grim, and I touched her arm. "You okay?"

She nodded. "I'll be all right. Mom hoped I could take Nana out today because she seemed so much better. And then I lost her again." Sadie fumbled in her purse for some cash and placed it on the counter. Nana had moved to another display and stood facing the jars of facial scrub flakes. She was shaking her head and muttering.

"Thanks. Is there something I can help you with?" I worried if Sadie could manage getting Nana home.

"No, it'll be fine." She gave a sad grin. "So long as I pretend I'm my mom and go along with Nana. We just never know when it hits her. See ya on Sunday, Miss Clark." Sadie went to Nana and took her by the arm. They left with Sadie assuring her they'd go straight home so Nana could take a nap.

The last thing I heard before the glass front door

glided shut behind them was Nana saying, "But I'm not tired."

"Everyone lives in someone else's shadow." The memory of Nana's lucid statement slammed into me hard. The hint about Melinda being in Charla's shadow made me pause.

I had a mental argument with myself as I went back to the workroom to study the promotional flyers that Sadie had picked up for me the week before. If I ever got to the point where I'd need an employee, I'd hire Sadie in a heartbeat.

Yet clearly Sadie's nana wasn't always in her right mind. How could I know for sure she'd been talking about Charla and Melinda and not another pair of students? Maybe she'd confused them with another pair of siblings. And it wasn't like I could come right out and ask Melinda about her sister. Even I had that much tact. Well, maybe not when it came to Charla's grieving fiancé, but then I hadn't really known him, and I wasn't trying to accuse him of anything, just get some answers.

If I was looking for a female killer, I couldn't rule Melinda out or the rest of the wedding party. I went to my desk and rested my head on my hands and closed my eyes, letting my mind settle back to that awful Saturday two weeks ago. It seems I'd gotten off track, chasing after leads like Mike and Robert instead of concentrating on what happened the day of the crime.

Melinda had said something about one of the

bridesmaids pulling a mean prank on Charla once before. I racked my brain. *That's right.* The bridesmaid had given Charla some candy with strawberry in it as payback for Charla borrowing a sweater without asking.

I dug through my desk to find the file for Charla's party. Di and I had used it when we made our suspect list, but I couldn't remember where I'd put it. When I finally found it, I flipped it open and scanned the names and profiles. *"Emily."* The onetime friend and roommate. She, like Melinda, knew Charla's schedule, her comings and goings. Both women seemed genuinely heartbroken over Charla's death. And if Sadie's nana had been right, maybe at least one of them was tired of living in Charla's shadow.

The funny thing was, I didn't recall seeing Emily at Charla's funeral. Did she stay away out of guilt?

———

"Ands, why are they all staring at us?" Ben muttered under his breath as I set the potato salad on the picnic table. The late-June air felt downright balmy, and I was grateful our group had managed to snag a great picnic spot under the pines at Greenburg City Park.

"It must be you." I glanced at the teenagers milling around the picnic area. A few had started a game of touch football, but another cluster of young people stood there looking at us, grins spread across their faces. "I'm too old to have a boyfriend. Most women my age already have the minivans and car seats."

"Ah, I see."

Oh, the depths of the male reaction. However, I wasn't trying to drop a really large hint about a diamond or setting a date. Not after the roller coaster of emotions I'd experienced while adjusting to the idea of Ben coming home from the road. My prayer time had increased a lot, something I'd needed anyway, but in the busyness of running the store, I'd started neglecting that area of my life again.

The pine branches swayed above us in the hot breeze, and the teenagers' shouts and laughter echoed around the park. The youth pastor and his wife were keeping an eye on the grill. Between the four of us and a couple of parents, we'd all keep an eye on the kids.

Sadie shot me a grin across the way and gave a half nod, one of her hands laced with a boy's—Kyle, I guessed. My throat caught. We adults had been cautioned to make sure none of the teens wandered off two by two. Not that Sadie would, but even I knew what it was like to be young and in love—or at least in love. And all of Greenburg knew about the famous Lovers' Oak, where scores of couples had carved their names over the years. The tree lay along a deep hiking trail that wound above the river's edge.

Ben moved to stack the plates at the end of the largest picnic table where we'd set up the main spread of food. I looked up from the opposite end of the table to see his smile hit me. My stomach's butterflies fluttered.

"Hey, Miss Clark." A voice at my elbow made me turn.

"Seth! Hi. You made it." I hoped my voice didn't sound like one of those bright, overeager adult voices. "Some of the guys are starting a football game. Later we'll have a water-balloon toss."

Seth dug his toe into the pine needles. "Er, I'm not good at football. I thought I'd hang out by the grill." He spoke to the potato salad on the table.

"Sure, whatever you'd like to do. I think a group is planning to hike the river trail later." I'd definitely hit the high-pitched-perky-adult-voice mode. *Blech.*

He shrugged. "Maybe." Seth seemed like he wanted to say more but shuffled off in the direction of the grill.

Poor kid. I didn't know how close he'd been to Charla, but if his family was anything like mine, he had to be taking it hard. Momma liked to use the old adage, "Still waters run deep." This seemed to apply to Seth. Maybe Ben could talk to him. Seth always arrived at church alone, and he was usually gone immediately afterward. I think either he walked or a family member dropped him off, but that was only a guess on my part.

"A kid from your class?" Ben opened the cooler and helped himself to a can of soda.

"Seth Mitchell. He's Charla's cousin." I watched Seth across the way, doing his head bob at something the youth pastor was saying. "I wish there was something I could do to help him. He seems so. . .lost."

Ben settled onto the picnic table bench. "That's a hard age. Half kid, half adult."

"He looks like he's got something all bottled up

inside." Now Seth trudged to a pine and sat down, leaning against its trunk. Instead of joining in the football toss or the other nearby conversation, he seemed content to be a spectator. He would glance around the picnic grounds then look at his watch.

"Do you think the pastor would talk to him?" Ben focused on Seth as well. "Or maybe I could."

I tried not to let the hollow sigh escape, but it did. "If Seth would be willing to talk. I've only seen him one Sunday since Charla died."

"Listen up, everyone!" the youth pastor called through cupped hands. "We've got some burgers 'n' dogs fryin' right now, and dogs'll be ready first. So start lining up."

Ben looked from the pastor to Seth. "I'll try to talk to him over lunch. Maybe break the ice a little."

I touched his arm. "That would be great. I've tried to talk to him, but he usually mumbles and turns red."

"You're a beautiful woman." Ben slid his arm around me. "If I was a young man, I'd be scared to death to talk to you."

"Ha!" I put my arm around him. "In teen years, I'm ancient."

We found a place in line and managed to get a burger apiece in spite of the teens that swarmed around the food table like feeding piranha. Ben scanned the group.

"Are you trying to find Seth?" I glanced from one cluster of teenagers to another.

Then I saw him.

Seth and two other boys stood at the edge of the hiking trail that entered the pine woods. He held a hot dog in one hand and was talking around a mouthful. The boys, who definitely did *not* belong to our group, kept gesturing toward the trail. Without a backward look, the three of them entered the forest.

"Ben—" I placed my plate on the nearest table and surrendered my lunch to the flies that waited.

"Let's go." He reached for my hand.

By the time the trees swallowed us up, we had lost sight of the three boys. "How did they disappear like that?" I could only see trail and underbrush. A brook gurgled somewhere as it made its way to the river. Birds called to each other in the treetops.

Ben squinted down the trail and into the woods. "I'm no tracker—I don't see where they could have gone off the path."

I had to trot to keep up with Ben. The trail split, one branch leading uphill and the lower one leading toward the river. "I vote we take the river trail, and if we don't find them once we get to Lovers' Oak, we should turn back."

We stumbled along the winding path, and sweat trickled down my back. This was not a smart idea. I should have at least brought my cell phone to call back to the main group and let them know where we were.

"I think we're almost there," Ben said after a few minutes. "Haven't been down this way in years." The last time was when he'd impulsively carved our names in the oak.

Soon we arrived at the most famous tree in Greenburg, the Lovers' Oak, once said to be a lookout post during the Civil War, although for the life of me I could never figure out how anyone could climb the thing.

There were the initials I remembered so well: *BH* +

AC. We'd been together six months, starry-eyed like a couple of teenagers and given to long walks in the park. I ran my finger across the bark. Myriads of initials, some obliterated by an angry knife after a breakup. I wondered if Momma and Daddy had carved their initials in the trunk or not. They didn't seem terribly romantic.

"Still there." I smiled.

"And so are we." Ben placed his hand over mine and raised it to his lips. "I love you, Ands." He took me in his arms. Where had Ben learned such impulsivity?

"I love you, too. And I've been praying a lot, especially about us." I forced myself to look into his eyes. "I couldn't and wouldn't want to think about being with anyone else."

His kiss made me remember the reasons I fell in love with him. His strength combined with his gentleness made me feel as though I could accomplish anything.

When he let me go, my cheeks flamed, and it wasn't from the humidity. I found myself grinning.

"Here we are doing what we didn't want any lovelorn teens running off to do." I forced myself to scan the woods.

"I know. We should try to find Seth, and if we can't, we should head back and tell Pastor." Ben took my hand, and we continued down the trail. As best I recalled, it ended at a small lodge and pavilion that the town rented out for parties and receptions, with a small dock for boats on the river. Another road from the lodge passed the park pool and led back to town.

At the edge of the clearing, I froze. Ben's hand pulled against mine. "Wait."

Two figures stood in front of two cars parked next to the lodge. Robert, the bereaved fiancé-lawyer, and a familiar-looking woman—one of the bridesmaids. Even from here, I could see her pleading expression.

"Why are we hiding?" Ben's voice sounded too loud. He moved toward the clearing.

I grabbed his arm and ducked behind a patch of undergrowth. "Hush—they'll hear you. That's Charla's fiancé and one of her bridesmaids. Emily, I think."

"So, they're talking."

"But who drives out to a deserted lodge just to talk? Maybe so they can talk where no one will hear them." I wished we could get closer so I could hear better. "Let me listen."

Across the expanse of lawn, drifting on the hot breeze, came a few snatches of conversation mingled with the sound of a locust hitting its full trill. "—you've just *got* to listen—" Emily's voice took on an urgent tone.

"—can't take the dramatics—" Robert took a step backward closer to his car and tugged on his tie.

Emily reached forward and touched his arm. "—won't say anything—"

"—enough to deal with right now." Robert shook his head.

"I would have said something sooner—"

Robert held his hands up as if to push Emily away

from him. "—calling or stalking won't work with me."

"—really need to talk to her. I've never seen her like this—"

"Ands, you need to stop this." Ben took my other hand, pulled me to a full stand, and forced me to face him. "These are people's private lives, and you can't make assumptions based on scraps of conversation. You're taking this too far."

"I *know* someone murdered Charla Thacker." I pointed to the pair by the lodge. "And I think he could have had something to do with it. Or maybe she did. Or both of them. What if Robert was seeing someone else?"

"Let it go. It was an accident." Ben paused and cleared his throat. "Jerry told me the lab results are inconclusive and prove nothing."

"What?" My throat constricted as if someone had clamped a vise around it. "How do you know this?"

"He said results showed strawberry in the scrub, but there's no proof it was put in there on purpose."

"Why didn't he tell me?" I wanted to sit down and cry. "And why didn't you tell me, either?"

Ben sighed. "I found out last night. Told Jerry I'd break the news to you."

"I don't know what I expected the lab to find. I'm not happy that I'm right." I watched Emily trudge to her car, her shoulders slumped. Robert wasted no time in spraying parking lot gravel from his tires and disappearing on the road to town. Whatever they'd talked about had made him aggravated enough to ruin his paint job.

"He wanted me to let you know, and actually, I hadn't thought about it since he told me last night." Ben caressed my cheek. "I'm sorry."

It wasn't that I feared as much for my business as I did at first, but my gut told me something was very *wrong* about Charla's death. Lab results proved there were strawberries mixed in the Cherries Jubilee, and I didn't understand why no one in authority believed me when I told them I didn't put them there. Well, actually I did understand. I couldn't prove anyone had a firm motive.

"We should head back." Ben turned to walk the way we came, and I followed, trying not to trip on an occasional stump.

What was Emily begging Robert about? Why wouldn't he listen? He had the look a guy gets when he's cornered by a woman.

What if he'd been having an affair with Emily? Had he put her off and gone ahead with his intent to marry Charla, and this action pushed Emily over the edge? But if that was the case, what man would go to a remote location to meet with a woman he thought was stalking him? No, that wouldn't work. Emily mentioned him talking to "her." Whoever "her" was, Emily sounded almost desperate.

Ben glanced at me. "I can smell your brain hitting overdrive from over here."

I managed a smile. "So much doesn't add up to me."

He stopped so quickly I almost ran into him. "It doesn't have to add up."

"I won't accept that." I crossed my arms.

"You can jump to conclusions without knowing the whole story. Look at us: We disappeared and ran into the woods. How do you think that would look to our group?"

"We were just looking for Seth," I said.

"We're also a couple in love," Ben fired back. "Do you think that sets a good example? What do you think some people would assume?"

"That's not fair. If you really think that, we shouldn't have gone into the woods. Besides, people who know us also know our standards." We continued our trek back to the picnic site.

"What about those who don't?" His footsteps pounded the trail next to me.

Sweat stung my eyes as I trudged beside him. "It's not the same."

"Oh, isn't it? You're making assumptions about people you barely know."

"So what is it I'm assuming?" I caught sight of the edge of the woods and a glimpse of our group beyond.

"A secret affair, a cover-up of some kind. A crime of passion." Ben took my hand as we left the woods.

"Yes on the first two." I wiped my forehead with the back of my free hand. "But on the third assumption, no. I think whoever did this planned well. Mike Chandler showed me that much."

I wanted to scream once we reached our picnic table. Not only had my plate been pitched out with the rest of the trash, but Seth glanced up at us as he chowed down on a thick slab of watermelon.

"Would you look at that?" I whispered, thankful the rest of the group appeared oblivious to our absence and arrival.

Ben shook his head.

—

Melinda, Emily. Emily, Melinda. I chewed on a piece of fresh beef jerky that Di had dropped off at the store on her way to take the kids to the library. If I ate much more jerky, I'd be ready to moo, but Di had been so enthusiastic about using her food dehydrator I couldn't resist. The afternoon was still young, and the lunch rush was over. This time all three customers had come and gone by two, and the hours until closing time stretched ahead of me. I couldn't expect more business on a Wednesday, and I'd stewed over the whole strawberries situation since the picnic on Saturday.

I had to dig deeper into both Melinda's and Emily's relationship with Charla. I still remembered Sadie's nana and her reminiscing about Melinda and Charla. But then there was that secret meeting between Emily and Robert at the parking lot. Emily had seemed urgent, desperate, almost passionate as she'd addressed him. If only Ben and I could have gotten a little closer to them. If only I could see Melinda, Charla, and Emily in their past, in black and white, untainted by people's opinions and hearsay—and in the case of Sadie's nana, impaired memory.

My daddy always said if you wanted to learn about something, you could find it in a book. Of course, this was before the Internet. I decided to take his advice, close the store for the afternoon, and head to Greenburg's public library. They probably carried back editions of Greenburg High's yearbooks. Daddy also said the past often dictates the future, and if these three women's pasts converged somehow, maybe looking at their younger selves would shed some light on them.

Yet Ben's admonition to mind my own business rang in my ears, and I almost decided to give up the idea about Charla's death being more than an accident. Almost.

However, my inner radar blipped louder than Ben's words, so I jumped in my Jeep and went to the library. After securing six years' worth of yearbooks dating from the year that Charla started high school until Melinda graduated, I settled down at a table then opened my notepad.

Echoing whispers and shushes made me look up to see Di and my nephews heading in my direction. She grinned.

"Hey there. Just getting the boys from Young Readers Camp. I think they're ready to explode from all their pent-up energy. Wish I could bottle it. Sherri Martin invited them for ice cream with her kids."

"Wow, I can see they're excited." Stevie darted around the corner of a bookshelf after his younger brother.

"Sherri's meeting me out front to pick them up." Her gaze fell on the yearbooks. "What's that?"

"Greenburg High's yearbooks." I tapped the cover of the nearest volume. "I'm doing some sleuthing."

Stevie returned with Taylor in tow, and Di reached for Taylor's hand. "Thanks, Stevie, for snagging him for me. Taylor, don't you run off like that again. I tell ya, they love stories, but once it's time to go. . . Can I give you a hand?"

"Of course. I need another brain to pick besides mine."

"I'll be right back." Di marched off with the boys to the front of the library, leaving me with a stack of high school memories on the desk in front of me.

Without waiting for Di to return, I flipped open the volume from Charla's freshman year and checked the index. As I expected, Charla had at least half a dozen appearances in that first year's edition.

I jotted down which clubs she belonged to and who she appeared with in candid shots. Charla was all smiles, looking forward to a future bright with promise. A lump swelled in my throat. She had no idea then that she had only eleven years left to live.

Sometimes Daddy says I'm too philosophical for my own good, but I suppose I get that from Momma. Would I have lived the past eleven years of *my* life differently if I would have known the future? Trouble is, none of us do, which is why we either spend our lives at the edge of the cliff being scared to jump, or else we grab on to the hang glider and fly. Charla flew.

Like her or not, a person couldn't say she didn't. And what had I done?

I'd skittered at the edge and watched others do what I didn't dare. Not finishing college. Not sticking with a business. Ben and Di both pegged me on that one.

Lord, I'm sorry for wasting time. And now look at me. . . . I'd treated Ben so callously, thinking of my own self before him. Love was supposed to be the most selfless, the most patient, the most kind. I stopped my train of thought. It wasn't the time to mull over my life and my choices. My quiet time would come later. I found myself looking forward to those moments of listening for guidance and wisdom in my life.

Charla's smile beckoned to me from the pages. She didn't deserve what happened to her, no matter how people felt about her. Whoever sabotaged that scrub still walked around, free and alive with a future ahead of them. The question was, where did that murderer lurk?

So, what'd you find out?" Di slid onto the chair across from me. She looked worn to a frazzle, and I suspected she needed this break.

"Nothing new, really." I pushed away somber thoughts about my personal life. "I'm making a list, year by year, of Charla's time in high school—and Melinda's and Emily's—to see what activities they participated in, who their friends were, and maybe find some foes."

Di's gazed probed my face, and she frowned. "You okay?"

I shrugged. "Yeah, I'm just realizing some things about myself. But I don't want to talk about that right now. We need to get through these yearbooks and get as much information as we can."

"Okay." Surprisingly, Di decided not to push me by asking any more questions. I did fill her in, though, on why I was concentrating on Emily, as well.

"Who'd have thought? Robert cheating on Charla?" Di shook her head.

"I. . .didn't say that. . .for a fact," I stammered. My face grew hot. Here I was, sounding like a biddy in a beauty shop, clucking about the latest news. "It's a theory I have but nothing for sure. Why else would Emily meet him out there? Plus, remember that get-together after Charla's funeral? That woman named Kaitlyn still cared for Robert."

"So Robert's not squeaky-clean either. . . ."

"No, nobody is actually. But that doesn't make him a murderer, either."

"Okay. We'll stick with the innocent-until-proven-guilty idea." Di reached for a yearbook. "What am I looking for again?"

"Any pictures of Charla, Melinda, or Emily." I opened the next album in front of me. "I'm not sure what I'm looking for, exactly. I'll know it when I see it. Especially look at any candid shots. Those might not be labeled with captions, but usually that's when someone's guard is down."

"You got it." Di saluted. She turned a few pages then paused. "Would you look at that hair? I can't believe we did our hair that way."

"Ha. At least you didn't have the late '80s big hair like I did." I cringed at the memory. "Sometimes I wish Momma would burn those pictures from junior high."

We chased ideas round and round, and through our digging in the yearbooks, we discovered that Emily, Charla, and Melinda seemed to be quite popular. Charla's senior yearbook was the most vivid. National Honor Society, Historians Club. Added to that, she performed the coveted role of the Greenburg Hornets mascot besides making the homecoming court. She'd already scored a coup her junior year by being crowned homecoming queen.

The other two girls had done well, too. Emily had been nominated one of the class clowns, but she stood out in her own right. Even sophomore Melinda shone as the lead for the Drama Club's fall and spring plays. She also excelled as one of the youngest ever varsity drum majors in the marching band.

Then I saw a picture that made me gasp.

A candid shot of Melinda and Charla walking arm in arm down a crowded hallway. Charla's now-familiar smile, wide and bright. Melinda's expression of adoration for her older sister. What got my attention was another individual who didn't know she'd been captured on film.

Emily leaned against a locker in the background. The black and white shot made empty black holes of her pupils as she stared at the passing sisters. A shiver plucked my spine.

And Sadie's grandmother had spoken of everyone living in someone's shadow. Maybe Nana had been on to something; only she couldn't have known she spoke of Emily.

"Di." My voice croaked. "Look at this." I swung the book around so she could see the picture, tucked in a lower corner of the page in a collage of photos.

"Now that's downright creepy. She looks ready to rip someone's face off."

"You can't mistake that kind of expression." I wished I could somehow enter the photo and hear the conversations swirling through the hallway.

"A hot glare doth not a murderer make." Di spun the yearbook back, and I studied the picture some more.

"Right, I agree. But think about it. She didn't know

anyone was taking that picture. Probably thought she wasn't even framed in the shot." The image of Melinda and Charla niggled at me, too. "I feel like we're looking at something, but we don't know exactly what just yet."

Di closed the final yearbook and looked at me thoughtfully. "You did say something about Emily having a mean streak?"

I nodded. "The day Charla died, Melinda mentioned a prank that Emily pulled, giving Charla some candy that caused a mild allergic reaction as revenge for borrowing a sweater. Sounds petty to me."

"What if, though, something *had* gone on between Emily and Robert, and Emily just wanted to hurt Charla for going through with the wedding?" Di drew a design on the notepad between us. "What if Emily planned this elaborate prank, only it backfired?"

"So she freaked when Charla died and didn't say anything about what she did, figuring it would fall back on me and look like an unfortunate accident." I rested my chin on my hands.

"You know, you might be on to something." Di looked thoughtful.

"Except I can't go blazing into Jerry's office pointing fingers at Emily, or Melinda either, for that matter." I stacked the yearbooks in a pile. "He said he'd think about someone tampering with the scrub, but I still have no evidence."

"We need to dig deeper on Emily. . .and Melinda, too."

I smiled at Di. "I'll find a way. Melinda seemed

warm enough the last time we spoke. I think now would be an appropriate time for me to call and at least see how she's doing."

Di asked, "What about Emily?"

"I'll figure out a way to talk to her, too."

On Thursday morning, I called Melinda's cell phone and left a breezy message, asking how she was and telling her that I'd thought of her. Which I had. And if Melinda crossed the bridge I'd built between us, maybe I could find out more about her and Charla. Talking to her, though, wasn't like barging into Robert's law office. Also, I cared about Melinda's well-being. The memory of her and Charla's happy faces as they walked down the hall had kept me awake.

Momma always called me the sensitive one, and about 3:00 a.m. I hated that "gift" she said I'd been given. Sometimes being empathetic caused me to interpret people's feelings the wrong way. I'm only human. So I prayed until I fell asleep—about Charla's murder, about the store, and about Ben and me. I prayed for his safety, too, as he was out on another trip.

I was still in a mental fog while I went about my morning routine at the store. A few tourists stopped and bought a basketful of products and gathered business cards to give to their friends. The thought of repeat orders made my heart sing.

When the bell above the door clanged, I looked up and froze. I hoped my expression didn't look as shocked as I felt. Seth Mitchell stood in the doorway like a deer in the middle of the road looking at oncoming high beams. The summer brightness outside backlit him in a silhouette.

"Um. Miss Clark. Hi." He tugged at the waistband of his baggy jeans.

"Hi, Seth." I stayed where I was behind the counter. "How are you today? Were you looking for a gift? For your mom? Or someone special?"

Oops. Not quite the right thing to say. A red flush tinted Seth's neck and spread to his ears. "Um, no. Not exactly."

"Well. . ."

"I'm looking for a job," Seth blurted. "I could help you make soap, or sweep floors, or take care of the outside of the building, or paint or something."

The poor guy. Here it was, on the brink of Fourth of July weekend, and any jobs for teenagers to be had were already taken. I wondered what made Seth choose my business.

A car pulling into the parking lot outside made him turn to face the front window, and I looked to see who'd driven up, as well. Melinda Thacker. This was very convenient for me. Ever since Di and I had looked through those yearbooks yesterday, I felt like I'd had a glimpse inside Melinda. What she still must be going through. The very thought of losing Di almost made me sick to my stomach.

Seth's face went from blush pink to ghostly pale when Melinda entered. "Hi, Mel."

"Hey there." She stopped and stared at her cousin. "What brings you here?"

"Looking for a job." He started digging at the floor with the toe of his sneaker. "Thanks anyway, Miss Clark." Seth left the store without another look at Melinda, almost as if he were being chased.

I realized then that I hadn't turned him down or even talked to him about a job. Not like I was in a position to hire anyone.

Melinda turned back around from watching him leave. Her eyes looked unusually bright this morning. "What's with him?"

"I don't know." I shook my head. "He said he was looking for a job."

Her laugh sounded shrill, and her hands trembled as she grasped her purse. "Well, I'm glad you called me. That was nice of you. People aren't calling a lot anymore. It's like Charla's just gone, and no one understands what a big hole she's left."

At that, I nodded. "My aunt Jewel ran off and left without a word when I was little. She and my momma were best friends. I was only six, but I still remember Momma crying. It was almost as if my aunt had died."

"That's not quite the same, but losing someone suddenly. . ." Melinda swallowed hard and fumbled with a sample bar of soap at the counter. "You just don't think about how it will be, trying to get used to life without them. The out-of-town guests leave, grass starts growing over Charla's grave, and people stop asking about her. It's like they all know she's gone. . .and it doesn't matter anymore."

"If it helps to know, I've been praying for you and your family."

Melinda shrugged. "Thanks. God doesn't seem very close right now. Not for a long time, really. Not since youth group in high school."

"All you have to do is talk to Him." Churchgoing is part of the Greenburg way of life. Knowing God and talking to Him? Let's just say some of us are still trying to figure that out, and I could see Melinda was no different than a lot of us.

"Emily's been super, though." Melinda gave a slow smile, and my senses snapped to attention. "She's been there at every turn. I never realized what a good friend she was to both of us."

Melinda fell silent, shifting her weight from one foot to the other, and as she looked around the store, it dawned on me that Melinda hadn't come to Tennessee River Soaps since her sister died. Here she stood in the very room where Charla had breathed her last.

"Do you want some coffee? Or maybe we could go somewhere else? I can close for lunch." I'd need to start finding an assistant to run the store if I kept closing like this.

"That sounds like a good idea." Melinda's face grew as ashen as Seth's had when he saw her enter the store. "I didn't think it would be so hard to come here. Nothing personal, you know. Your store looks and smells beautiful."

"No offense taken. It took a lot for you to come here, but I'm glad you did." I smiled at her, trying to put my finger on her demeanor. More than grieving over Charla, it seemed like a fresh pain, a new worry had come over her. Was it just the fact that she was getting used to life without Charla? I hoped to find out over lunch. Maybe this unexpected encounter with Melinda was an answer to prayer.

14

I saved Charla's life once." Melinda took a sip of her sweet tea and set her glass back onto the same water ring on the table. The lunchtime noises at Honey's battled for my attention, and I had to lean forward in the booth to catch her words.

"What happened?" I figured I'd let Melinda talk. Maybe this was good for her, and after all, I'd offered to listen.

"She was fourteen. I was twelve." Her face took on a faraway expression as she stared out the window at the crowded parking lot. "She had just started high school, and I wanted to follow in her footsteps. We had stopped at the corner store on the way home from school. I remember still being jealous she was at the high school with the older kids, and she was nice enough to buy me some Ring Pops to make up for it. It's crazy, isn't it, the things that mean so much to us when we're younger? She bought a new brand of candy bar for herself and started having a reaction. Peanuts or something in the filling. She didn't know. Thank God she had her EpiPen with her when her throat started closing up. Not like. . ." Melinda's eyes filled with tears. She dabbed at them with a clean napkin. "I still don't understand what happened."

"I don't either." My next impulse was to tell her about the strawberries in the scrub, but I stopped. I could not afford to let that information out. Not now. *Wise as a serpent, harmless as a dove.*

"So here we are." Melinda's even gaze probed me, and I blinked, not breaking away. I had nothing to hide, nothing to be ashamed of or apologize for. Again, I had the feeling of not quite seeing all there was to see about Melinda. The music twanged in the background, something about a cheatin' heart.

"Yes, here we are." I decided to venture a question. "Do you think someone hated Charla enough to kill her? From what I understand, she was popular yet not well liked."

Melinda's face blanched. "That's a horrible idea. People were jealous of her, but I don't think anyone would do something so cruel. I don't see how they could have. . ." She blinked and looked away, a tear streaming down her cheek.

"I'm sorry, but I had to ask." I decided not to risk asking any more questions that might upset Melinda more.

Her expression smoothed itself over, and she focused on me once again. "Have you ever done something you thought you'd never do?"

"I've never thought about it. Can't say as I have, that I know of."

"I have." Melinda grabbed a fresh napkin and again dabbed at her eyes. "Emily tried to help, but she couldn't. Not with this."

"Does it have to do with Charla?"

Melinda shook her head. "No, not really. This

disaster is of my own making. Yup, walked right into this one with my eyes open."

Esther, the best lunchtime waitress at Honey's, appeared at our booth. "Got two specials right here."

We started eating, and Melinda didn't offer any more information.

I did venture to say halfway through my meal, "Melinda, I want to help you."

"No one can help me."

A sigh wanted to force itself from my lips, but I stopped it in time and concentrated on my grilled chicken strips and salad.

"Why did you come to see me today?" I tossed the question out. Sure, I'd called Melinda and left a message, but she could have simply picked up the phone to call me back.

"You're a nice person with a good heart. You're a big sister, too." Melinda grabbed another napkin. "I miss mine. And I never realized how much until now. So I knew you would understand."

Lord, what do I say? This was becoming much more than a hunt for clues and motives for killing Charla Thacker.

Melinda continued. "My parents are great. But there are just some things I can't talk to them about." She shook her head.

"Dessert, ladies?" Esther stopped at our booth again.

I wasn't ready for our meal to end. Not quite yet. "Sure, I'll have a piece of the chocolate-chocolate cake and a cup of coffee."

"Great choice." Esther looked at Melinda. "What about you?"

"The strawberry pie."

"Another good choice." Esther spun on her heel and left.

I smiled at Melinda. "Is any dessert ever a bad choice here? I'll pay for this later, but I'm in the mood for some of Honey's chocolate-chocolate cake. Besides, eating salad and cake cancel each other out, right?"

The corners of Melinda's mouth barely turned up. "I know what you mean."

Again we were left staring at each other, and I wondered if staying for cake had been a good idea after all. Melinda's sudden reticence baffled me when compared to her previous flickers of emotion.

We started on our desserts, and I broke the silence. "I'm sorry you feel that you can't talk to your parents."

"I'm an adult with adult problems." Melinda took a bite of pie. "And I don't want it to seem like I'm trying to get attention, especially after what happened to Charla."

"But they're your family. . . ."

"That doesn't matter. I've disappointed them, unlike Charla. I should have been the one to die."

"Don't you talk like that." The divine chocolate-chocolate cake had lost its appeal. "I don't know you very well, but if there's one thing I do know, every life has a purpose."

Melinda studied the parking lot again. "Sometimes I'm not so sure." She shifted on her seat and took a deep breath.

She had started with the half revelation then withdrawn again, and I thought about leaving. I wanted to help her but wasn't sure she'd truly welcome help. Some people thrive on drama, and I remembered her from the yearbooks as being the artistic, musical one.

"I. . .I don't feel well. . . ." Melinda grabbed her stomach. "The pie probably wasn't such a great idea." Her face had taken on an ashen tone; her brow began to bead with perspiration.

"Melinda, are you okay?" I glanced at her half-eaten slab of strawberry pie, and my first thought was an allergy. *No, not again*. . .and with me right here across the table from her.

"I don't. . .please, whatever happens, don't call my parents." She slumped over in her seat. "Oh, it hurts. . . ." Diners looked in our direction.

"Hang on. I'm calling 911. I'll be right there behind you." I grabbed my cell phone and dialed for help, my pulse pounding in my throat the whole time.

Once I found a parking place at County Hospital, I hurried to the emergency room. "Please, I'm looking for Melinda Thacker. She was brought here by EMS."

The desk clerk nodded. "She mentioned someone was coming for her."

"Can I see her? Is she all right?"

"I believe she's in radiology right now, but you're welcome to have a seat."

I would wait for her and not abandon this poor young woman in her hour of need. She didn't want her parents called, and I almost decided to ignore her request. But no, she was twenty-three, not a child. Instead, I prayed. This was not the afternoon I had pictured.

During the next hour, I mulled over our conversation. Melinda had shown up not long after Seth had arrived at the store. Her grief seemed to run deep, and she clearly found herself in a battle that made her cry out to me, of all people, for help.

At last, Melinda appeared through one of the doors. Her red and swollen eyes widened when she saw me. "You're still here. You didn't have to stay, but it was awfully sweet of you to follow me."

I nodded. "I didn't want you to be here by yourself, and since you didn't get a chance to call anyone. . ."

Melinda gave a small smile that didn't reach her eyes. "No, I didn't." She held a piece of folded paper. "Could. . .could you give me a ride back to Honey's to pick up my car?"

"Sure, of course." We left through the sliding double doors and headed to my Jeep. Melinda remained silent on the trip through downtown Greenburg and over to Honey's Place via a side street.

"So," I said at last, "are you okay? What was wrong? Do you need to get a prescription at the pharmacy or anything?"

Melinda shrugged, and a strand of her hair wafted across one cheek. She brushed it out of her face. "I'll be all right. One of the ER nurses is phoning my prescription to the pharmacy, so I'll pick it up on the way home." She bit her lip and turned to the open air rushing past the Jeep, but not before I saw a tear leak from the corner of her left eye.

I pulled up next to her car waiting in Honey's parking lot. Melinda grimaced as she hopped from the seat of the Jeep.

She slammed the door. "Thanks for listening. And for coming to the ER. Not many people would do that for someone they don't really know."

"You're welcome. If you ever need to talk, please, call me." I couldn't let her leave without offering a listening ear, even if I couldn't read her very well.

"I might take you up on that." Melinda gave a flicker of a smile and turned away.

As I drove off, I glanced down at a piece of paper on the seat. I unfolded it. Melinda's ER discharge paper. The diagnosis read, "Threatened AB." My heart thudded, my curiosity piqued. But it was none of my business.

I circled the Jeep around and stopped at Melinda's car. "Hey, you left your paper."

She lowered the window a fraction. "Huh?"

I waved the paper at her eye level. "You left this."

The window glided down farther. Melinda snatched the paper. "Thanks. Gotta bring that to my regular doctor." She had the window up again before I noticed the paper cut on my index finger.

All the way home, her diagnosis burned into my brain. What was going on with this young woman? What couldn't Emily help her with? It made no sense to me.

Once home, curiosity overcame me. I logged on to the Internet, pulled up my favorite search engine, and typed "threatened AB" in quotations. My stomach dropped into my feet when I scanned the results.

A term that describes a pregnancy in which there is bleeding and/or cramping, also known as a threatened miscarriage.

I clamped my hand over my mouth. *Oh, Melinda.*

15

And that's how I found out." I sat perched on the hood of my Jeep watching Ben change the oil in his pickup. "I never should have looked at that paper." My heart broke for Melinda. I'd wanted to call her a dozen times in the last week but didn't.

The Fourth of July afternoon sun radiated down on us. If I didn't get off the Jeep soon, I'd fry. If only Ben would hurry so we could get to the river for the town party.

He slid out from under the front of the truck, rose, and dusted the dirt from his jeans. "Your curiosity's going a mile a minute, huh?"

I nodded. "I'm just wondering who the father of Melinda's baby is. Not that it's any of my business."

My mind hit overdrive. "What if. . .what if she and Robert. . ."

Ben looked at me like I had grown a third eye. "What do you mean?"

"Melinda told me that Emily had tried to help her. What if Emily went to Robert on her behalf? You yourself said that Robert wouldn't meet in a deserted place with someone who was stalking him."

"True. . ." He rubbed the sweat from his forehead with the back of his hand. "But then it wouldn't be so secret if Emily knew, too."

"I'm not saying the scenario makes sense to me,

either. I still think Robert had something to do with Charla's death, and this would be a motive, but if Melinda was pregnant with his child, then getting rid of Melinda would be more logical. That is, if he didn't want the scandal of a child by another woman smearing his name. And *maybe* that's what made Mike Chandler so mad. Robert cheating on Charla." I huffed and took a sip from my bottled water. Its coolness slithered down my throat and gave me an instant headache. "Ow."

Ben wiped his hands then removed the cap from the top of the engine's oil tank. "You're making an awful lot of assumptions, though. Better slow that train of thought before it derails."

"I don't understand why Melinda came to me. I did offer to talk if she needed someone, but quite frankly, I'm surprised she took me up on the offer."

"You've got a giving heart and a good set of ears." Ben crossed the short distance between us and gave me a quick kiss. "Lips, too." He slid his hand over my cheek.

I grinned. "You seem to appreciate that." Did I mention I loved it when Ben came home? When I didn't think about being scared, the thought of having him around thrilled me. By the end of the summer, I'd be seeing him a whole lot more.

Then I had a sudden thought. "Hey, if Melinda wanted to break up the wedding, she sure had a great motive. What if *she* somehow messed with the scrub?"

"Stop." He stepped over to his truck, opened the large jug of oil, and started to pour. "You don't know that."

"But I keep thinking about what someone told me,

that we all live in someone's shadow. What if Melinda resented that. . .and losing Robert?"

"I can appreciate what you're trying to do, but you know Jerry's going to need some proof." Ben replaced the oil cap back on the engine, then slammed the hood on his truck. "You know that's what he's going to say."

"I know. And I have no evidence that points to Melinda or Emily as the source of the break-in." I shook my head.

Ben took me in his arms. "Enough about that for now." When he held me, it was easy enough to forget things. "I need to tell you some news of my own."

"Oh?" He'd been so full of surprises lately, I should have been bracing for another one.

"I gave my notice to the company. I'll be free of them within a month and back here for good." The smile he gave made me freeze. "I prayed about it, and I know it's time."

"Wow." A jumble of thoughts tangled in my mind. "That's. . .fast."

"Is that all you can say?" Ben caressed my cheek.

"I–I'm glad. It'll take some getting used to, but I know I won't worry about you like I have, out there on the road." Ben. Home. All the time. So soon. When he held me, though, change didn't worry me, as long as we were together.

"Jerry and I talked it over one night. He said he'll help me on the house when he has the time."

"You know Jerry—he's so busy." I gestured with my hand. "But what will you do for work?"

Ben shrugged. "I've put out a few feelers. Someone was talking about having a bus service between here and Memphis, so I might drive for them. I'd be home nights and most weekends. Plus there's Greenburg Auto. They need a good mechanic, and I could get back up to speed."

"Wow again. But it doesn't matter to me what you do for a living." That's where some women get shallow. They want status, and it reminded me of Charla dumping Mike Chandler. Aloud, I continued. "Because I'm proud that you have initiative. Lots of people say, 'Oh, I'd like to do something one day,' and they put it off and never try. But you do. And that's one of the things I love most about you."

He leaned his head toward mine. "Well, I want your daddy to know his little girl is going to be taken care of, one way or another."

"Really? I haven't been a little girl for years." I loved seeing the dimple in his cheek as he smiled at me. "I'll try to relax and be taken care of for a change."

"You should. I don't see anything wrong with you being independent, but independence doesn't mean we don't need anyone at all." He swallowed and blinked.

"Is that what you thought? That I didn't need you?" I hugged him.

"Maybe." His voice sounded hoarse.

My heart hurt at the idea of the pain I'd caused him, without thinking, without realizing it. I knew Ben speaking these words and choking up cost him something.

"Ben, I need you. You anchor me like no one else in this world can. I might go off on a wild tangent, but you bring me home again. And with Charla dying at the store, it's really thrown me." I sighed and hugged him again. "I know you haven't always agreed with some of my ideas, but you've been there for me."

"That's good to hear." Ben kissed the top of my head. "Whoever said falling in love was easy hasn't tried staying in love. Now, that's the hard part. Well, not hard. I mean it's hard work."

"It is, isn't it?" I had to admit. "But I wouldn't trade this for the world. And I mean that with all my heart."

"Same here. And when I don't agree with you, it doesn't mean I don't love you."

"Of course. But I still think Melinda had something to do with Charla's death."

Ben shook his head and laughed. "You just don't give up, do you?"

I merely grinned at him. "You ought to know me by now."

A cloud of dust streamed behind Ben's pickup as we headed for the Tennessee River. Greenburg always does the Fourth of July up really big, and this year was no exception. We'd have to hurry to get a good place by the Tennessee River Bridge to watch the fireworks display at dusk. All I'd heard last week was how people couldn't wait for the town tailgate party. Di's husband,

Steve, had fashioned a new portable grill for their family spread, and Di had been bragging about it the past week. Like I said before, you bring on the food, you bring on the people. Church, family, and food—that's Greenburg.

"Hang on." Ben shot onto the dusty side road worn down by other rivergoers over the years. Teenagers and old folks alike had blazed a dirt trail that wound downhill and flanked the river on both sides.

I glanced back at our cooler, sliding back and forth in the bed of the truck. Hopefully the lid hadn't popped off the potato salad container inside. We snaked down the trail between the trees that provided relief from the heat if not the humidity, then zipped out into the late afternoon sunlight.

Ben managed to find a decent spot that gave us an unobstructed view of the sky above the bridge, where they'd shoot off the fireworks at dusk. Long shadows slanted across the site, and a few families already had their grills lit and coals glowing. Some kids chased each other around with water balloons.

I saw Di and Steve two vehicles down from ours. Di waved, her grin wide. "Hey y'all, you made it."

"It wouldn't be the Fourth if we missed this!"

Ben dragged the grill out to the end of the tailgate. I saw to the cooler and also saw that my potato salad had indeed tumbled across the inside and spilled across the ice packs.

I turned to break the news to Ben. "Sweetie, I hate to tell you, but my potato salad ended up all over the cooler. At least the burgers are fine."

"Uh, no, they won't be."

"Why not? If we just have burgers and chips without salad, that's okay."

"We only have chips and soda." He sheepishly kicked at a nearby rock. "I forgot the charcoal."

"Oh." Mr. Never-Forget-the-Details Ben forget something as vital as charcoal? I shook my head and shrugged. "We'll figure something out."

Ben gave a longing look at a nearby grill, where someone else's perfectly shaped burgers sizzled. "I can't believe I did that. The Fourth won't be the Fourth without my Bongo burgers."

Ben makes the best burgers in the world. I don't even know what's in his so-called Bongo burgers, exactly, but anyone who's tasted one doesn't care. He mixes his secret ingredients and pounds the meat with his hands, hence the name Bongo burgers. An Independence Day without Bongo burgers would be as unthinkable as Independence Day without barbecue, the "1812 Overture," and fireworks.

"Don't worry about it. Maybe Steve will make room on his grill for our food." I glanced in their direction. Di was yelling at the boys about something—probably trying to keep them out of the river, which gurgled yards away from our vehicles on the dirt road.

"Okay." Ben sighed and picked up the container that held the burgers. "C'mon. Let's go beg for some grill space."

I slipped my arm around him. "You know, I don't

mind. Life's full of crazy stuff, isn't it? And we don't have to figure everything out."

"You've got that right." He clasped his arm around my waist and gave me a half hug. "As long as I'm with you, let the crazy stuff come."

"Same here. As long as we have Bongo burgers."

We ambled the six yards or so over to Di and Steve's truck, where all the makings of an outdoor kitchen had been spread out behind the vehicle.

"Please, help us." I pointed at the burgers Ben carried. "We didn't bring any charcoal."

Steve looked at me as if I were nuts. "No charcoal? Here, throw 'em on." He took the meat from Ben.

"Thanks, man." Ben clapped him on the back. "I owe you one."

"So where's Momma and Daddy?" I squinted along the river road.

"Momma wasn't feeling well, so she said she and Daddy were going to stay home, order pizza, and watch the Nashville fireworks show on TV." Di opened the cooler and fished out some cans of soda for the boys. "Here. Y'all don't throw the empty cans on the ground."

"We won't, Mom." Stevie nudged Taylor. "C'mon." They shot off to a group of their friends not far away.

"Pizza?" I shook my head. "That doesn't sound like them."

Di fanned herself with a paper plate. "Momma said it was too hot to go out, and I don't blame her."

As we watched the river flow past, we also noticed someone else. Emily stood out against the red, white, and blue of our fellow revelers. She made a solitary figure in her fuchsia sundress as she strolled along the riverside in our direction. The last time I'd seen Emily was that horrible day Charla died. Well, when she'd known I'd seen her. I couldn't quite count the time I saw her at the park by the lodge, talking with Robert-the-Grieving-Fiancé.

"Look, there's Emily," I mumbled to Di, all the while looking at the top of their cooler. "I'm going to talk to her."

"I'll come with you." Di linked arms with me, and we approached the young woman.

"Hi, Emily." I gave her my best smile. "I was wondering how Melinda's been."

She looked at me quizzically, her pale eyes standing out against her summer tan. "Oh, you're the lady who runs that soap store."

I tried not to read anything into the "soap store" comment. "Yes, that's me. I helped Melinda get home from the hospital the other day. I've been concerned about her." Which was definitely the truth.

A shadow crossed Emily's expression. "I have been, too. She won't hardly talk to me, though. I tried to get her to come today, but she wouldn't budge from the couch."

"She's been through a lot." I nodded. "First Charla, now this. . ." I glanced at Di, whose face remained sympathetic. How to get out of this hole I'd started digging for myself?

Emily shrugged. "I feel awful about what happened.

I did what I could to help her, but. . .I mean, hindsight's twenty-twenty, they say, yet I didn't suspect. . ." Her eyes rounded as she looked behind us at the path.

I glanced over my shoulder to see Robert-the-Grieving-Fiancé approaching.

"Em! There you are!" Robert's stride screamed confidence. I blinked at his attire. Who'd wear khakis and a polo shirt to a riverside Fourth of July bash? At least, in Greenburg, that is. I have to admit, a woman would have to be barely breathing not to give him a second glance.

Emily's face flamed. "Hey there, um, Robert. I, um, was looking for you, too."

Robert gave me the megawatt actor's smile. "Miss Clark, is it? I trust you're still in business?"

"I am, thanks."

"Were you able to learn more answers to your questions?"

I looked him in the eye. Only the faintest shadow remained from where he'd had his black eye. "Actually, I'm finding out more answers with every passing moment."

He took Emily gently by the elbow. "Ladies," he said to us as he escorted her away, and they ambled in the direction of the bridge.

16

After Emily and Robert had disappeared in the crowd, Di turned to me and squealed like she was in junior high. "Did you see that? What was going on there?"

I shook my head. "I have no clue. Except he doesn't seem like he was grieving as much anymore. But then you just can't go on appearances, can you?"

"What was that Emily said about hindsight and wishing she could have done something to help?

"I don't know. I couldn't tell if she meant the scrub or about helping Melinda in her trouble." Through the swirl of revelers, I glimpsed Emily, who glanced back at us. The couple headed uphill toward the main road. "But I sure wish she'd stuck around for us to ask about the baby."

"Not with Robert right there." Di turned on a heel and squinted at their little picnic site. "I hope Steve's paying attention to those burgers. Otherwise, we'll all go hungry if he scorches them."

"Ben will be crushed if his Bongo burgers get ruined." I looked at the table full of goodies Di had spread out. If I knew Ben, he'd volunteer us to move our food down with theirs. Domestic Di hadn't left out anyone's appetite. She'd chased everyone away from the potato salad, cold tossed pasta, pickled okra, and watermelon but hadn't stopped the boys from plowing through a bag of potato chips.

Shouts from the river made me look in that direction. A few kids were flinging water at each other with plastic cups, and their joyful play made me smile in spite of my confusion about Emily. The innocence of childhood refreshed me after the lies and scheming and heartache I'd discovered these past weeks. Not in myself, but in the townspeople, who on the surface seemed successful and happy.

"Why don't you and Ben join us, since you're not grilling? We have a ton of food." Di plucked my elbow, and I turned back around.

"You don't have to twist my arm. My potato salad was ruined." I frowned.

"Oh, that's terrible. You used Momma's recipe, too, didn't you?"

"I did. Finally tried to make it after all these years. Maybe I'm not hopeless in the kitchen, and now we'll never know."

"Hon, you're not hopeless, just ignorant. And it's never too late to learn."

"Ha. Funny. I can cook enough to make a mess. And dessert. I can do that." I smiled at Ben, who'd settled onto a folding chair next to Steve. "I'll be right back." Not like I had much to bring back to Di and Steve's spread, but at least the kids would appreciate more soda and chips. And we needed the extra pop-open canvas chairs.

I headed to Ben's truck and let the merriment of Greenburg flow around me. Tonight I could almost forget the break-in, Charla, Melinda, and the whole drama surrounding the store. Right. After seeing Emily, I didn't know what else could happen to turn the situation on its head.

It was still too early to start hashing over the interaction I'd just witnessed. I knew I couldn't very well go back to Di's picnic spot, pop open my chair, and sit staring out at the river while I tried to think. For some reason, if I got too quiet, people asked questions.

"Hi, Andi." Trudy from Higher Grounds coffee shop blocked my path. She held out a red, white, and blue flyer. "Here. This is a fireworks safety and accident prevention guide."

"Oh, thanks. I'll pass this on to Di. I think she and Steve let the boys bring sparklers this year." I folded the flyer.

"I've missed seeing you at the drive-through window in the morning." With her long hair drifting in the breeze and gauzy tunic over a peasant skirt, she reminded me of a long-lost flower child.

"I've kind of been on a budget lately, because of the store and all."

Trudy nodded. "I completely understand. I was so mad this morning I almost wanted to spit nails."

"What happened?"

"Someone broke into Higher Grounds last night. Not only did they trash the place, but they smashed two boxes of coffee cups and threw coffee grounds and beans all over the floor." Trudy blinked hard. "Did they tear your place up that bad?"

"No, they sure didn't." My heart went out to Trudy. "Will insurance cover the damages?"

"It will, but it's the principle of the thing." She extended her arms out to the side and waved, the sleeves of her tunic flapping like a pair of wings. "I mean, c'mon people, if you're just there for the money, take it and leave everything else alone."

"I'm really sorry to hear about that. But no, they only took some money from the drawer. Nothing else was disturbed. Or, I should say vandalized." Shadows from the trees crossed our path, and I could see Trudy without squinting as much.

"Sorry, I didn't mean to dump on you like that." Trudy sighed. "I knew you could relate though, because of the incident at your store."

"Don't worry about it." I waved off her concern. "That's why we small-business owners need to stick together."

"Speaking of which, you really ought to join the chamber of commerce. It would be good publicity for you—and exposure." Trudy fanned the stack of flyers in front of her. "Plus, you get to do community service and hand out things like this."

"I might do that. But Roland Thacker's the chairman of the board."

"Don't let that stop you. Roland knows business is business. I'm sure he doesn't blame you for what happened." Trudy glanced over at a nearby family. "Well, on I go with my safety crusade. Stop by the shop when you can."

"I'll do that." I tried to smile at Trudy, but she had already flitted off again like a butterfly to another flower. She must be on a perpetual caffeine buzz, as much energy as she possessed.

Once I picked up the cooler and the bag of chips from the truck, I managed to tuck the fold-up camp chairs under one arm and head back to Di and Steve's area.

Ben hurried to meet me. "Hey, you should have asked me to come with you instead of trying to drag all this back on your own."

I grinned. "Thanks, but I didn't really think about that. Here." I let him take the cooler that had bumped and slid behind me as I dragged it along. "How are your burgers doing?"

"They're fine." His dimple winked at me from his cheek.

"At least dinner is saved tonight."

Soon we had our seats clustered around Steve's grill and watched him remove hot sausage links, ribs, and hot dogs and place them in a pile, a virtual heart attack on a plate. Di corralled Stevie and Taylor away from their friends and the water's edge. She efficiently broke out the Wet Wipes while Taylor protested.

I grinned and took a hot link, plus some of Di's salad, then returned to my chair next to Ben's. His eyes caught mine.

"What's going on?" He took a swig of soda.

"What do you mean?" I started on the hot link,

and the spicy bite made my lips tingle.

"You have that look on your face."

"What look?" Couldn't a person just eat without talking up a storm? I tried to smile at him, but my mouth burned.

"That look that tells me you're anywhere but here." Ben looked out at the river. "Today's a day to sit back, relax, and celebrate our freedom, not carry the weight of the world, or at least the weight of Greenburg."

I sighed. "Di and I saw something earlier that really surprised us, and I'm trying to figure out what it all means. Emily, one of Charla's bridesmaids, meeting up with Robert here at the riverside and leaving together. They looked awfully friendly."

Ben nodded. "Okay. We know they know each other. Just remember, you might only be seeing part of the story."

"I know that, and I'm trying to keep that in mind. But it doesn't add up." If I kept on like this, I'd give myself a royal headache. "If Melinda and Robert had been an item, what's going on with Emily and Robert now? Especially after having such a heated argument the day of the youth group picnic?"

"Maybe they made up and he's giving her some law advice. Or they're going to another get-together. Or maybe having dinner somewhere else instead of getting bitten"—Ben slapped his arm—"by mosquitoes near the river while waiting for the fireworks display to start."

"Okay. I get your point." I glanced toward Di.

Maybe she had some bug spray. She'd already lit a citronella candle. "Just because people hang out together doesn't mean anything romantic is going on."

But my women's intuition radar was going off again. Maybe it was from growing up in a small town where new couples always get thrust under the town's microscope, with every smile and handhold and glance scrutinized. Assumptions weren't fair to Emily or Robert. Just because he appeared to have moved on pretty quickly didn't mean he had anything to do with Charla's death.

Ben took my hand and made me look at him. "So what about us?"

"Oh, yes. Definitely something romantic going on."

Ben's eyes sparkled in the twilight that glowed on the river. "I'm glad to know that. Because once I'm home, we'll have plenty of time to spend together."

His love crossed the space between us, and I felt it wrap around my heart. "I can't wait. And I mean that."

"Just do me a favor."

If he'd asked me to fly to the nearest star I'd have tried. "What's that?"

"For tonight, drop this crusade of yours. Concentrate on us, and leave other people's troubles and worries far away."

I squeezed his hand and realized he'd been the talkative one tonight. It always meant something for Ben to open up like that, so I replied, "Tonight, that's a promise. I love you, Ben."

"And I love you, too."

The first *whoosh* of fireworks being set off echoed from the bridge, followed by a spangle of lights in the dusk. Then came the ground-shaking *boom*. Ben slid his chair closer to mine and put his arm around me. Tonight, regardless of what else had happened, my world was perfect. I'd be like Scarlett O'Hara and worry about the other situation tomorrow. Or at least until the fireworks' glow died away.

17

Despite my promise to Ben while we were at the river, I tossed and turned after settling in for the night. When I did sleep, I dreamed of Emily and Robert, her in a wedding dress and him in a tuxedo, while Melinda chased them. She was crying and held a baby in her arms. Then the baby disappeared. Emily and Robert's laughter made Melinda sprout wings and fly away. I stood there, my hands tied with clothesline rope, while Ben had his back to me and couldn't hear my cries for him to do something.

Wouldn't a shrink have a field day with *that* dream? I laid there in the dark and stared at the evil clock that told me it was only three thirty.

Finally I threw off the covers and went to the medicine cabinet. This was definitely the last time I ate a hot link so late at night. Heartburn. I found a container of antacid, took some, then decided to get a cool drink.

The air conditioner rumbled in the window as I passed it on the way to the kitchen. Tonight my normally snug home felt yawning and empty. I thought of Di's home, filled to the brim with love and clutter and chaos. The clutter and chaos would drive me nuts, but I wouldn't mind a home at least filled with love. And controlled chaos. My independence, once worn like a badge of accomplishment, now seemed rusted and old.

How many times over the years had Ben hinted that I should ask him to come home? I couldn't blame him for not being straight-out forthright about what he wanted, and maybe my prickliness had shot him down before he'd had a chance to speak.

What if I had said, "Ben, please come home so we can start our life together" three or four years ago? I wouldn't be here, renting my great-aunt's old shotgun house and listening to the air conditioner rattle the walls in the middle of the night.

"Right now you're alone. Just like Melinda. Just like Charla. Just like Emily, even though she thinks she's found someone."

So I poured myself a glass of ice water, and I prayed. For Melinda, Emily, even Robert, although I didn't hold too high an opinion of him. And for Ben and me, of course. I'd been having more of these heart-to-hearts with God, when I wasn't just begging for His help to keep my business afloat. What kind of a relationship is it when the only time the one you love talks to you is when he or she wants something? So I was trying to rip my focus from my fear about life, love, and solving a murder, and focus on how much God wanted to be a part of everything I did.

The trouble about living in a town like Greenburg is, as I said before, church is something you do. It's easy to get involved in the whole flurry of activities and warm fuzzies, but when the bottom drops out of your world, all the going-through-the-motions won't hold you up.

Maybe that's what I realized again once I'd finished praying. All I knew is that by 4:00 a.m., I was ready to crash. That, and I knew I had to call Melinda as soon as it was good manners to call someone.

That time didn't arrive until nine in the morning. My cell phone's battery was dead, so I looked up the number for the Thacker residence and called from my house phone for Melinda. I couldn't leave for the store until I'd spoken to her. Not after my fitful night's sleep and only one cup of coffee. In fact, I decided to drop by Higher Grounds and splurge on a high-octane mocha.

"Oh, I'm sorry but she's not here," came a woman's voice. "Melinda hasn't lived here for quite some time. She lives with Emily and Ch. . .with Emily."

This was news to me, since I didn't run in the same circles as the Thackers. I ran in circles enough trying to operate a business and still make sure my parents knew I loved them.

"I'm the one who's sorry for disturbing you, ma'am. I'll try Emily's then."

Of course this meant I needed to go to the store and go through the records from Charla's party to find Emily's phone number, so I headed out before I got distracted.

I frowned when I passed Higher Grounds and saw the CLOSED sign. Poor Trudy. She was probably cleaning up the damage from the break-in.

Which made me think of my own encounter with

the thieves. Nothing had been disturbed in my store. If anything, this confirmed to me that the break-in couldn't have been linked to the others. Why trash some stores and leave mine intact? It didn't make sense.

Once I arrived at the store, I opened for business. Maybe a tour bus would take a scenic route to Nashville, pass through Greenburg, and happen upon Tennessee River Soaps. A girl can dream.

I found the file from Charla's party and looked up Charla's home number. When Melinda answered, her tone sounded guarded.

"Melinda, it's Andi Clark. Um, I was calling to see how you were."

"I'm doing well, thanks. For a while I was pretty tired, but I'm back to work."

"That's good to hear." How could I ask without prying or playing dumb? I didn't want to stoop to out-and-out subterfuge by asking a question I already knew the answer to. "I have to admit, it was pretty scary seeing that happen to you."

"I—I'm so glad you were there. You don't know me very well, but you even showed up at the hospital, and that was very kind of you."

"You were in trouble, and I wanted to help."

"Thanks." The line hummed.

"I still mean that, Melinda. I know you've been through a lot and—"

"Like I said, thanks. But I'm fine now. Life goes on, you know. I've just got to figure out what that means for me."

"So do we all. Well, I'll let you go." At the risk of sounding pushy, I ventured another probe. "If you need anything, I'm here."

"Thanks." The line went dead.

Right, she was fine, just like my quarterly sales had gone through the roof after a *great* second half of the month of June.

The rest of the morning crawled. For some reason that tour bus I hoped would drive by never stopped, so I downloaded some Internet orders and breathed a prayer of thanks.

A hunch niggled at me. What about Robert? Did he know about the baby? Ben would tell me just to leave it alone, but I had to know. I wasn't sure if it made any difference in motivation for murder, but perhaps I could learn something more about Melinda and Emily and where they stood with Robert.

I packed up my Internet orders to ship and headed to the post office. A side trip by Robert's law office wouldn't take long. Once I had my customers' orders safely on their way, I drove to Robert's office. The guy probably already thought I was loony after my last meeting with him, when Di tagged along, but I really didn't care.

His receptionist greeted me with the same flat tone she'd used before. "He happens to have a few minutes, if you *must* speak with him."

"Yes, I must."

She disappeared behind the walnut door and emerged a moment later. "Mr. Robertson can see you now."

I smiled my thanks and entered Robert's office. "Good morning, and thanks for seeing me again on short notice."

"How can I help you, Ms. Clark?" Today he wore a periwinkle button-down shirt, its long sleeves rolled up on his forearms. Great color. Brought out the shade of blue of his eyes. So very Mel Gibsonish.

"I have some family law questions I was hoping you could help me with."

"Go right ahead." That charming smile emerged again, the same one he'd used with Emily the night before. Maybe he just smiled like that at all women. I was glad Ben didn't. I'd probably want to bop him on the head if he did.

"Well, what if an unmarried couple were to, um. . ." Oh, this was going badly. My face flamed. "If a woman were to get pregnant out of wedlock, is she under any obligation to tell the father of the child?"

"No, not to my understanding. There are some who would insist she must, but there's no legal obligation."

"Even though she could in turn serve him with a paternity suit if she so chose."

Robert nodded. "It doesn't sound quite fair, does it?"

"I imagine that would be a tough situation to be in, a man fathering a child he knows nothing about and still being legally obligated if the mother so chose." I met his gaze evenly, and he returned my stare without blinking.

"I agree. Which is why couples shouldn't enter into

relationships lightly." He wore a quizzical expression.

"So she could go after him if she wanted to, even get a DNA test if need be?"

"That's correct."

"Well. . ." I tried to choose my words carefully. "What if she miscarried a child? Would she have to tell her, um, the father of the child?"

"As I said before, she's under no obligation to tell him."

"Wouldn't you like to know if you'd fathered a child?"

The expression he gave confirmed the suspicion I had: The man thought I was bonkers.

"Ms. Clark." He shook his head. "Is this for your own personal information or someone else's?"

My throat tightened and my face must have been as red as the sunburn on my nose. Surely he didn't think—

"No, no, no. Not for me." I coughed. "I'm asking on behalf of a friend." This sounded worse and worse. *"It's not for me; it's for a friend,"* a mocking voice whispered in my ear.

"Of course, of course." He smiled at me again, and I tried not to look him in the eyes but instead looked at his perfect nose. "If you'll excuse me. . ."

"Thanks for your time." I fled the office. What a pointless errand. Embarrassment didn't begin to cover what I felt. My last glance back at Robert showed he'd already dismissed me from his world.

Once in the security of my Jeep, I took some deep

breaths and realized that even if I tried to go back and explain the reasons behind my questions, I'd be betraying Melinda's private business. I realized I should explain to Ben just in case anyone around town looked at him askance. People who knew us, though, knew our standards.

And from Robert's reaction, I didn't worry about him mentioning my babbling questions to anyone. After all, there was such a thing as attorney-client confidentiality. Of course, I wasn't exactly his client, but he surely thought I was a little. . .off.

I leaned my head against the steering wheel and stifled a scream. It was then I noticed a buzzing coming from my purse. My phone! I'd forgotten I'd set it to VIBRATE. I scrounged until I found it.

"Andi, it's Pastor Tim. I'm afraid I've got some bad news."

My heart dropped into my feet. "What's wrong?"

"It's about one of your Sunday school students."

"What happened?"

"Seth Mitchell has been arrested with several of his friends. An anonymous tipster placed them at the site of the latest break-in. In fact, it sounds like there's multiple charges against them."

"Oh, no. I've been worried about him. I was hoping we could help him somehow."

"I know you have. I guess they also found some evidence linking him and his buddies to the crime."

"Thanks for letting me know. I'll be praying for Seth. And for his family."

"Thanks, Andi."

I flipped my phone shut and tried not to cry. *Lord, I feel so inadequate. I didn't do enough.*

18

As best I knew, Seth remained in jail the next few days. Come Sunday morning, my high school Sunday school class was abuzz. Evidently he and his friends had several charges against them and their families couldn't afford bail. Either that or they wanted to teach their kids a lesson.

One student blared aloud about the three young men being transferred to the county jail as of Friday. "They're all eighteen. That means they're *adults*."

I tried to whistle through my fingers to grab their attention. A few of the students swiveled in my direction, and the others followed suit. "Y'all, I know you like to help the *Greenburg Dispatch* spread news, but let's not start their trial here." Although I had several questions of my own I'd like answered.

Once the class settled down, we lost no time in taking prayer requests. Seth was at the top of the list. A few somber-faced kids wondered aloud if they could have helped him.

Sadie spoke up. "But what if some people don't want help? I mean, we all hear the same lesson every week and can read the same Bible. So why doesn't it stick, if you know what I mean?"

"I do know what you mean, Sadie." I opened our study book. Trust Sadie to come up with the most insightful questions I'd ever heard from an eighteen-year-old. "Maybe some people don't know how to ask for help, or if they do ask, we miss it."

The thought struck me like lightning as we sat in our circle. Maybe that's why Seth had dropped by the store. Asking for help, silently, and I hadn't a clue. Of course, Melinda had shown up, so it wasn't as if I'd had a chance to talk to him before he ran off.

I continued, "So maybe that's why it's okay not to be shy to ask each other the hard questions. 'Are you okay?' 'Can I pray for you?' 'Do you need something?' Because lots of times, maybe people don't know what they need. And if we're Christians, shouldn't we have some answers? We ought to watch out for each other—without smothering each other, of course. Those New Testament Christians were told over and over again to love each other deeply."

Oops. A few blank expressions and the sound of imaginary crickets chirping met my ears. Maybe I'd gotten a little too serious for them. But a few faces, deep in thought, told me I might have said something that made sense.

I also realized I'd done what I could to help Melinda. I would back off and pray for her now, pray that someone would enter her life whom she would listen to and trust. She'd certainly had her trust broken, if in fact Robert had already moved on.

So we prayed for Seth and the other requests and continued our lesson. After class, the students said their good-byes, and I entered the hall of churchgoers. Where was Ben?

I hadn't seen him since the Fourth, which was

strange. In all the years he'd been on the road, we usually spoke every day, even if we didn't get to see each other. And two days without a phone call and Ben still in town—well, something just didn't feel right.

Our relationship (when I wasn't freaking out over commitment) felt like cozy relaxation on the front porch. He never chased me. I never chased him. Some couples seemed to thrive on drama, but not us. Yet today, for some reason, I knew I *had* to talk to him.

I saw him standing at the end of the corridor with Jerry. He stood in his best jeans and pressed shirt, his Bible tucked under his arm. The light from the side entryway caught the blue in his eyes that I could see from a distance. When he looked in my direction, I gave a half wave. There went his dimple.

When I reached the end of the hall, Ben slid his arm around my waist, then released me. "Hi, pretty lady."

"Hi yourself. So what have you been up to?"

Jerry cleared his throat and excused himself.

Ben blinked. "Er, not much. I had to go up to Jackson."

"Jackson?"

"Yeah, some stuff for the trucking company. Exit interview. They helped me with a résumé.

"That's nice. You didn't mention they helped employees with that—or about-to-be-former employees."

"They do." He tugged at his shirt collar, although he didn't wear a tie. "Oh, I think that's the music starting."

We walked into the sanctuary, and I'd never felt so far from him while standing so close. Ben had evaded me. Sure, he was normally on the quiet side, but even Ben was good for more conversation than what we'd just held in the hallway. Maybe it was just my imagination.

His gaze remained fixed straight ahead during the service. I quieted myself. He didn't have to spill his guts if he didn't want to. If he was in a quieter mood than normal, so be it.

After the service, we entered the parking lot, and Ben stopped me before I headed to my Jeep. "I'm leaving tonight."

"Oh. I didn't think you were going until Tuesday."

"Someone else canceled, and this is a good trip. I'd be foolish not to take it. I'll get a little more money in the account." He gave me a quick hug and a kiss. "See you when I get back."

"Okay." I nodded absently. He walked off just like that, leaving me standing and staring after him. I wanted to run after him, but I didn't want confirmation that a wall had risen between us, even an imaginary one. Ben usually told me when he expected to be home.

I flipped open my cell phone and called Momma, hoping she and Daddy were already home from church.

"Hey, Momma." I did my best to sound cheerful. "You and Daddy going to be home?"

"You come right out, hon." Her warmth wrapped itself around me. "Diana and Steve aren't coming today. One of the boys upchucked in the church parking lot, so they're going straight home. And me and your daddy have all this food waitin' for someone to eat it."

"I'll be there in fifteen minutes."

—

"I am so glad I'm not spending my time cleaning the bathroom, sheets, or little boys' pajamas," Di said as she breezed into Tennessee River Soaps on Monday morning. "I think if I had to stay home today, I'd go stark raving mad."

"So, um, who's taking care of my nephews?" I pointed at Di. "Surely you didn't just leave them."

"Of course not. Steve took a personal day off from work today and told me to get out of the house for a while." She grabbed a bar of Glorious Gardenia soap and inhaled, smiling.

"That was sweet of him."

"He does things like that." Di grinned at me. "I think Ben would, too."

I nodded and went to restock the displays. While I didn't have any new product yet, I wanted to make shoppers think there was plenty of merchandise when they walked into the store.

"What is it? Spit it out."

Nope, no fooling Di either. "Ben's been acting strange ever since the Fourth. And we had a great time with y'all. I don't get it."

"What do you mean?"

"He hasn't called me. I got his voice mail every time I called between the Fourth and yesterday. He barely said ten words to me at church yesterday, and then he left, just like that, last night." I snapped my fingers and restocked the strawberry soaps, but not without a shudder.

"Well. . .maybe he's got a lot on his mind."

"I know. He probably does. He's leaving a relatively secure job and coming home to who knows what."

"God knows."

"Yes, He does." I moved to the other end of the store to check the floral soaps. "Which is why I'm trying not to sound too lovelorn, like I'm waiting for him to call after a first date. We're so beyond that now, after seven years."

"Like I said, he's probably got a lot going on. He knows you're there for him."

I nodded. "Okay. Enough about me. I need your help." We both cracked up at my statement.

"So what else do you need?"

"Fall's coming. I need some new soap scents." I grabbed my notepad and pen from the counter. What I really wanted to do was find a way to help Seth, but there was nothing I could do. Not right now, anyway. "Summer's halfway over, and I need to look ahead to fall. So help me brainstorm."

"Pumpkin," Di blurted.

"Who'd like pumpkin-scented soap?"

"Lots of people."

"Well, I'll keep it in mind. Maybe something with spice in it." I jotted down "pumpkin," put a question mark next to it, and moved on. "What about something cool and brisk that would remind someone of a fall night?"

"Peppermint?"

"That's it—how about a nice refreshing foot soap? I hadn't thought of that before. A foot scrub. Good going, Di. Maybe I could make that one for November."

"Thanks." She pulled a plastic sandwich bag out of her purse and opened it. "Want some dried bananas?"

"Sure." I popped a handful into my mouth and crunched on them. She'd finally switched from making beef jerky to drying fruit. "Okay, more fall products. I'm thinking of doing three to start with. Pumpkin— with reservation. Peppermint—definitely. And. . . ?"

Di went into my office, dragged out my desk chair, and plunked herself onto it next to my stool. "I'm thinking. . .maybe something with apple? Or cloves. . .Autumn Night. . ."

I rested my head on my hand and sighed. Along with Ben's behavior and Seth's trouble, summertime and strawberries refused to leave my head. "Not to change the subject, but I've been thinking about my cherry scrub. Maybe whoever tampered with it didn't think the strawberry seeds would be discovered."

"Okay, this is miles away from soap. Sort of."

"I was thinking that, as far as I knew, the scrub container wasn't dusted for fingerprints. Jerry has the bowl of Charla's scrub. He took it so they could test it. Hang on for a second." I slipped back to the workroom, put my gloves on, and took down the ill-fated cherry scrub container.

Di followed me into the workroom. "So where are

you going with this?"

"If they didn't expect anyone to suspect foul play, maybe—just maybe—their fingerprints are on the lid, on the container. They wouldn't have bothered to wear gloves. We could be looking at some valuable evidence here."

"You need to bag it."

"Right." Once I grabbed a trash bag and stuffed the container inside, I glanced at my hand. "You know, this container has my prints all over it, too. Sure hope I haven't smudged any of the killer's prints since the break-in."

"Did you touch it a lot?" Di stared at the trash bag.

"Just to look at the scrub, when I sifted some strawberry seeds from the soap flakes awhile back." I could see the wheels turning in Di's head as I spoke. "Which brings me back to another big question: How would the killer get strawberries into a powdered form that would blend right in with the soap flakes?"

"Well. . ." Di scanned the room as if the answer were hidden near my workbench or in the storage cabinets. "Something that would leave the seeds behind, for sure."

"I already figured it couldn't have been strawberry essence, oil, or a gel. Not with those seeds in the scrub."

"How about mashed?"

I shook my head. "There was nothing in those dry flakes that made them look any different at first glance, not until I sifted them. Mashed would have still been wet and mushy the next morning. Plus, the flakes would have dissolved and there would have been a mess in the containers."

"So, dried."

I shrieked, then ran to the front of the store where Di had left her bag of dehydrated bananas on the counter. "Wait, I've got it. It's been in front of us the whole time."

When I returned to the workroom, I held up the bag to show Di. "*She* could have used a food dehydrator."

"Wow. It makes sense." Di held up her hands as if in self-defense. "But really, I didn't do it!"

"Right, you and most of the other women in Greenburg." I chomped on a few slices of dried banana. "Thank you, Di, for caving to this latest fad. So, *she* dehydrated some strawberries, tossed them in a blender—which happened *not* to grind up the seeds— then brought the powdered strawberries and dumped them in the scrub."

For the first time in a while, I felt closer than ever to figuring out the means this killer used to murder Charla Thacker. I felt very close to tracking down a killer who still thought *she* got away with it.

Di grinned. "So does this mean I can start giving you beef jerky again?"

"Moo!" was all I said. No way would I share this news with Jerry just yet. His reluctance didn't welcome my ideas. But I was determined to find some evidence he couldn't ignore.

19

So what if 75 percent of the adult women in Green-burg owned food dehydrators they'd purchased at Value-Mart? The store had discovered a huge marketing gold mine. I didn't bother to calculate how much the store made selling food dehydrators in Greenburg at nearly forty dollars each.

I bit my lip as I drove to the house Emily and Melinda shared. Maybe I could ask if either of them owned one. Wouldn't hurt.

Then I smacked my forehead. Di had been enthu-siastic about our breakthrough that morning, but neither she nor I had contemplated how I'd broach the subject with either woman. What was I thinking—that I'd just hop in the Jeep and head out for a friendly visit—uninvited—with two women I barely knew?

It would be extremely tacky of me to offer them some coupons for the store or free samples of bath salt. If they still considered me the source of the sorrow in their lives, if in fact either of them truly sorrowed over Charla, any reminders of how she had died would only cause their wounds fresh pain. Then again, if one of them was a murderer, it might force her hand.

I decided to show up, ask about Melinda, and watch to see what happened. When I arrived at their house, only one car remained in the driveway, and it wasn't Melinda's. I parked the Jeep behind Emily's vehicle and got out. The place looked cozy, with hanging plant baskets and a swing on the front porch. Music blared from somewhere in the back.

I rapped on the screen door. "Hello?" Maybe she'd hear me above the drums. I heard pounding feet on a hardwood floor growing closer.

Emily, clad in a T-shirt that was missing the lower half and ended miles above her low shorts, leaned against the doorway. "Oh, hey there. You looking for Melinda?"

"Yes, actually. I wanted to see how she was doing."

"Better." Emily smiled. "She's back at work already. Should get home later on, but she mentioned something about dinner with friends."

"Oh, okay." I swallowed and tried to think of what to say next. "I'm glad, then. Tell her I stopped by."

"I sure will."

Before I turned to go, I decided to take a chance. "Hey, I was wondering something. This might sound like an odd question, but have you ever used a food dehydrator? I'm, uh. . ."

"No way." She shook her head. "And if I never see one of those things again, it'll be too soon. Melinda got one awhile back. We had dried fruit and beef jerky coming out our ears."

I gave Emily a sympathetic smile as my heartbeat shifted into overdrive. "I know *exactly* what you're talking about. My sister has one, and she's always dropping off bags of her latest concoctions. I told her if she started passing out dried fish or bugs, she could forget it!"

"That's so gross," Emily said, laughing. "I feel your pain. After a while, both Charla and I were ready to pitch her dehydrator out on the front lawn and take a sledgehammer to it." Emily chuckled, a wicked light in her eyes.

"Ooh, such violence. Don't let my brother-in-law hear that. You'll give him ideas." I tried to sound glib. "Would you believe my sister is *still* dropping off bags of fruit? Just this morning she brought dried bananas. I've got to say, the pineapple is pretty good."

"You sound close to your sister." Emily's expression changed as a shadow crossed her face. "Melinda and Charla were, and since Charla died, Melinda hasn't been the same."

"You're worried about her, aren't you?" I was still trying to figure out if Emily was a true friend or the kind who played on a friend's struggles and used them to her own advantage.

"Yes, I am. I don't know how else I can help her. I suppose it's normal, what she's going through. . ."

I nodded. "After Charla, and the baby. . ." I shut my eyes and tried not to groan. *Big mouth.* The roar of a neighbor's lawn mower pierced the air.

When I opened my eyes, Emily was staring at me, her jaw lax. "You knew? I thought I was the only one."

"Yes. Actually, I thought that's what you were talking about on the Fourth of July, when I saw you. I found out purely by accident the day Melinda went to the emergency room." I shifted from one foot to the other. This wasn't how I'd planned the conversation. Come to think of it, I'd had no plan. I screamed a silent prayer for help out of this one. "Which is why I've been doubly concerned about her. Did she. . .lose the baby after all?"

Emily nodded and sighed. "She quit doing all the fun things she used to do, the things that made her happy. Piano. She dropped out of the civic theater's play. Even put away that stupid dehydrator. You know, she used to sing while loading that thing with fruit and stuff." Her sad smile touched my heart.

"Grief really rips people apart, doesn't it?" I spoke not from experience, but from watching those around me. A sigh came out and surprised me. "Well, I ought to go. I'm sorry for bringing up everything about Melinda. I shouldn't have said anything."

"Don't worry about it. I'll tell her you stopped by."

"Thanks, I appreciate it." I left without looking back, but I could feel Emily staring after me the entire time.

Different scenarios spun through my head and left me breathless. I had to force my attention to the road. Melinda, singing as she filled the dehydrator. Melinda, loaded down with a double load of grief. Melinda, forsaking two of the things she loved and excelled at, drama and music. Perhaps her acting abilities had served her well, and this new grief, a genuine grief at losing a child, had pushed her to a new level of vulnerability.

But what about Emily? What if she was tilting this situation to her own advantage, especially with me asking about the food dehydrator?

Evidence. Jerry needed evidence, and right now all I had was a pile of hearsay and hunches that pointed in one direction at two people. My head hurt, and I decided to cancel my budget diet for the moment and stop by Higher Grounds for the biggest, strongest coffee Trudy could fix for me.

The bell clanged when I entered the store, and Trudy welcomed me with a warm smile from behind the glass counter. "Hey there. I knew you'd be in eventually."

"Give me a double-shot mocha, extra tall, please."

"Whew, I sense a bit of stress in your voice. Right away." Her forehead wrinkled as she scanned my face. "You all right?"

"I'm just here to unwind for a little bit. It's hard to think and drive."

"Ha. Good one." The machine whirred as Trudy whipped up my coffee. "Do you need to talk about it?"

I shook my head. "Thanks, though." The way my mouth had run off earlier with Emily made me afraid to say anything else to someone who had no clue about the situation. Who knew what I'd blurt out?

An empty café table with a solitary chair waited in the corner of the shop, so I grabbed it before someone else did. The table gave me a view of Main Street and the life that rushed past the coffee shop.

"Here you are." Trudy set my cup on the table and

placed a plate of biscotti next to the steaming, tall mug.

"Oh, I didn't order the biscotti."

"It's on me. Enjoy." With that, she whirled on sandaled feet and went back to her post at the counter.

"Thanks," I called after her. The sip of whipped cream that floated on top of the coffee was very soothing.

I played out the scenarios before me. Sure, I could tell Jerry about the dehydrator. The idea sounded a bit farfetched to me, but what if it were true? He'd have to get a search warrant, go through a lot of questioning, and maybe get nowhere. Or I could try to get the dehydrator myself. I shot this idea down quickly. I didn't know much about the process of gathering evidence, but if I snooped around and grabbed it myself from Melinda's garage or something, any evidence probably would get tossed out just as if Jerry had blazed in there demanding to see the dehydrator. Like he'd try that.

Ouch. Now my head really hurt. A sip of the coffee made my senses perk up, and I realized the silliness of my ruminations. Emily didn't say Melinda had thrown out the dehydrator. She'd only said she'd put it away.

I downed my coffee and thanked Trudy once again. Time to pay a quick visit to Jerry for two reasons. I wanted to bounce my theory about the food dehydrator off him, and I wanted to see if he knew what in the world was going on with Ben.

But before I left, I ordered a tall double espresso for Jerry. Maybe bearing a gift of coffee would help.

It did. Besides the fact that the hour was creeping up on suppertime, Jerry looked worn to a frazzle when I showed up at the station. His hair stuck out wildly, overdue for a cut. But he lit up when he saw the covered cup of coffee I extended in his direction.

"Come on back. Tell me something funny. I need some humor today."

I followed him to his office. "Okay, this isn't a joke, but I think Melinda Thacker could have murdered her sister by putting dehydrated strawberries into my scrub. She has a food dehydrator. She had motive. Now I just need to find her means of getting into the store."

Jerry almost spit out his sip of coffee. "Try to be a little more direct, why don't you?"

"I bagged that container of scrub that I believe was tainted. I tried to tell you about it before. What if I bring it to you, plus you dust the bowl that held Charla's scrub? Now, if I can just find that food dehydrator Melinda has. . .or had. And if we find the same prints on all three. . .this would point to the means. And her opportunity is the break-in."

"Sit down." He gestured to the chair by his desk. "I see what you're getting at. But I need a motive." At least now I had his interest.

I grinned, sat down, and crossed my legs. "Melinda had no business being in my workroom. She never went in there the day of the facial. If her fingerprints are on the large container, she can't explain that."

"You're right." He took another sip of his coffee

and looked at the cup. "Good stuff."

"Oh, and I have a strong suspicion that Melinda Thacker was pregnant with Robert Robertson's baby. Charla's *fiancé*. That would be a strong motive right there to get rid of Charla." *Momma, you'd be so mad at me right now for talking like this.* My face flamed.

"Whoa." Jerry sank onto his desk chair. "That makes the whole scenario a bit more interesting."

"That's what I thought."

"But do you know it was Robert's?"

"I don't know for sure, but if it's true, I believe she loved Robert, and he didn't know about the baby. So when she sent Emily to talk to him on her behalf after Charla died, it was one final attempt to keep him. Which didn't work." I didn't add that I believed Robert had already moved on to Emily. Part of me wanted to warn the young woman, but perhaps that would be for another day. I'd already said enough. Even though Jerry had a right to know this information, I still didn't like hearing the sordid tale out loud.

"This is all quite a pile of information." Jerry steepled his fingers under his chin. "Your theory is possible, although it is a bit farfetched. I've got a medical examiner's signed statement verifying her cause of death as accidental anaphylactic shock."

"I've been around that a hundred times, but what if I'm on to something? If I can get you that evidence, can you at least check it out? If I'm wrong, I'm wrong."

"I have a budget that keeps getting slashed year after year, Andi." His sigh told me of the long hours he worked and the frustration with a system that wore him down. "I can't use taxpayers' money, performing investigations on every single unfortunate death in Greenburg. People have the craziest requests. One time, Doris Flanders wanted me to set up a stakeout for whoever was stealing her watermelons a few summers ago before she passed on." Jerry shook his head.

"I know you're in a tough position, but my gut tells me this whole scenario surrounding Charla's death is wrong." I felt like a bulldog gnawing on a bone. "I'll even do the legwork myself."

He gestured at the files on his desk. "If you don't mind, I need to see to a few things here."

I stood to leave. "Have you heard from Ben lately?"

He shook his head. "Nah. I usually don't, unless he's going to be in later than he planned. He just left last night."

"I know. Has he been, um, acting strange lately?"

"He seems a bit preoccupied, but I think that's understandable. Got some business in Jackson that has him tied up." Jerry paused, looked as if he was going to continue, then stopped.

"Okay." I could see his expression lock down, and I wasn't about to act like a pining schoolgirl trying to get scraps of information about the object of her affection. "If you hear from him, could you ask him to call me? Please? I think there's something wrong with his phone." I slung my purse onto my shoulder.

"Will do." Jerry had started writing some notes on

a legal pad. "Thanks for stopping by."

As I entered the late-afternoon heat, I allowed myself a grin. Jerry had listened. No, he wasn't going to launch an all-out investigation, but now I knew I had to hatch a plan to get that dehydrator. Or see if Melinda still had it.

Once I arrived home, the long evening hours stretched ahead of me. Seth came to mind again, so I called the county jail. Since I wasn't Seth's lawyer or family, I couldn't speak to him. I didn't even know if the message I left got through. I tried, though, and that was something.

I tried calling Ben, too, and ended up listening to his voice mail several times. My cell phone had only one message, from Di, asking about what happened with Melinda and Emily. Tonight I didn't feel like calling Di back. I'd already talked myself out brainstorming with Di, interviewing Emily, and then talking to Jerry in his office.

The next morning, promptly at eight, my home phone rang with a collect call from the county jail. I accepted the charges.

"Miss Clark, it's Seth Mitchell." I heard shouts in the background. "Could you please come to the jail? Visiting hours start at one. I really need to talk to you."

20

The only time I'd ever been to jail was in another lifetime that was high school, when my Criminal Justice Careers class took a tour of the county lockup. At the time I'd been toying with the idea of studying criminal justice in college. For some reason I changed my mind, but today as I sat in the jail parking lot, kitty-corner from the county courthouse, the whole setting came flooding back to mind.

I filled out some paperwork and had my ID verified and my purse checked. Once I was escorted to the visitors' room, I waited outside until my name was called shortly after three. An officer pointed me to one of several steel tables in the room. On one side was a chair for a visitor, and on the other a chair for the individual in jail. Security was minimal, but strict protocol had to be followed. I took a seat and waited along with other visitors, each of us at our own table.

Seth entered with three other men, and he wore standard county-issue jail clothes. He was not hand-cuffed but trudged into the room, his head down. I saw a light go on in his eyes when he sat down across from me at the table. I followed instructions to keep my hands on the table.

"Miss Clark." He showed me an inkling of a smile. "You came."

"Of course I did. We could have talked on the phone, though."

A flush shot through his cheeks. "Probably, but I needed to talk to you in person."

"About what?"

"I—I'm the one who broke into your store." The words shot out with rapid-fire delivery. "The other guys had nothing to do with it. It was just me."

"Why are you telling me this now?"

Seth shrugged. "I couldn't go to church and look you in the eye, knowing what I did."

"Did you talk to your parents about this?"

Another shrug. "Dad's got his own family in Jackson now. Mom's working. I know she cares, but. . ." He blinked and stared at the table as he spoke.

"Why didn't you say something before?"

"I couldn't." His voice sounded flat.

"Why? What are you afraid of?"

"I was only holding up my end of the deal."

"What deal?" I clamped my lips together, realizing I'd started to sound like an inquisitor. *Let the kid talk.*

"Brandon and Marcus and me only planned to get into one store, Giant Games. Supposedly there was plenty of cash in the office. Marcus said one of the managers owed him some money for a game he returned, but the guy wouldn't give him a refund. So they said we would just break in, get Marcus his money, or at least a game he wanted, and we'd go."

Seth paused and glanced around the room, but none of the other visitors and incarcerated individuals seemed to pay us any mind.

"So that's what you did."

"But once wasn't enough. And they said once I was in with them, I couldn't get out, that we were all in this together." Seth's flush deepened. "Um, plus, it was kinda cool to have some money for a change, if you know what I mean."

I nodded at that. "I've been in tough financial straits before. I'm there now. But Seth, why? And those other business owners—their places were trashed."

"I know, I know." Seth picked at something on the tabletop. "Brandon and Marcus started getting back at some people who gave 'em a hard time. I didn't think it was funny."

"But back to my store." My heart went out to the young man. "You didn't wreck the place."

"Like I said, I did this alone." He swallowed hard, and he finally looked me in the eye. "Miss Clark, I really messed up. Bad. I didn't plan on things going this far. For all I know, my mom's glad I'm in jail."

A niggling inside told me now was my chance. "Seth, your life can be different. It's not too late even now."

He shook his head. "I tried that church stuff. It didn't help. And some of those kids aren't any different than the ones I hang out with."

"I'm not talking about church attendance, or going to all the activities, or doing good deeds instead of bad. I mean, God has a plan for your life. There's no one else like you. And He really wants to show you what that plan is."

The sounds of the visitors' murmuring voices were swallowed up by my pulse pounding in my ears. I didn't feel adequate for this. Maybe this was the youth pastor's job, but Seth hadn't called him. He'd reached out to me. Wasn't this what the Sunday school class had prayed for?

"I don't know. I don't really want to be a preacher or anything like that."

"You don't have to preach. But I know for sure God has something special for you to do."

Seth shrugged. "I've got a record now. My lawyer says I'm looking at real jail time. A few years, at least. Maybe it's not that long to you, but my life should just be starting."

"It *is* just starting. You can start fresh. Now. Ask Jesus to forgive you, and you can start living for Him now, even if you're in jail. No matter what lies ahead, God will be there to guide and protect you."

"Why do you care? I heard you were only teaching the class at church for the summer."

"God made you, Seth, and so I care. I'm not the only one who does. Your Sunday school class cares, too. We prayed for you on Sunday."

"That's just great. Now everyone really knows what a loser I am."

"You can begin again. God loves you."

"I wish I could be sure about that."

"Start talking to Him, Seth. I know they'll get you a Bible or something here."

"I. . .I think I'll do that. I don't have much else to do."

My watch told me I only had a few minutes left. "About the store. . .maybe I could talk to your lawyer or something. I think you need another chance, Seth. And I think you need some new friends."

"I don't know if talking to my lawyer would help. You're right about the friends thing. Marcus and Brandon already got bailed out. I'm getting what I deserve, though."

"Why did you break into my store. . .alone? If they didn't get you to break into my store, why'd you do it yourself?"

"I. . .I didn't do it myself. Someone made me break in."

A knot twisted itself in my throat. "Who?"

"My cousin. Melinda Thacker."

I tried to inhale but couldn't. Pay dirt. All the signs kept pointing. I'd just found the right direction.

"She saw me and Brandon and Marcus breaking into some store late one night a couple of months ago. She said she'd turn us in if I didn't help her. So I had to help her. Alone." Now a pair of tears dampened Seth's cheeks, and he looked like a lost little boy. I let him continue.

"Melinda said all I had to do was break in and make it look like a robbery. She stayed in the back room while I went up front to get the money from the register. At the time, I didn't get why Melinda said she had to come with me to the store that night. But then when I heard about Charla. . ." He gulped and rubbed his eyes. "I went back and wrote KILLER on the window. I was mad and sick and. . .I didn't know what to do. . . ."

I didn't have children, but I did have two nephews I'd do just about anything for, and my heart broke for the young man sitting across from me. "Oh, Seth." But I stayed frozen where I was, my hands on the table and a guard standing by the door, watching all of us.

"But who would believe me if I told them? I didn't want to get caught, so. . ."

"You said nothing." My stomach churned. I'd skipped breakfast and now regretted it. "I wish you'd talked to me."

"I tried. That day I asked about a job." He wiped his eyes, and I pretended not to notice.

"Except Melinda showed up."

Seth nodded. "So I beat it, and I knew she wondered if I said something to you about the break-in."

"Did you tell your lawyer?"

"He's one of those public-defender guys. He doesn't care. He gets paid whether he wins or not. And the DA? He'll probably say I'm trying to get the charges lowered by making up a story."

"Seth, I believe you." I looked him straight in the eye. "I don't know if it helps you to know this, but I believe Melinda intended to kill Charla, and she *used* you to help her carry it out."

"Thanks, Miss Clark." He wiped his rapidly blinking eyes as the guard approached.

"Time's up, Mitchell."

I stood, hoping Seth would glance my way again.

"Remember. . .I believe you, Seth. If I can help you, I will."

With that, he nodded, and the guard walked him to the cell-block door. I left the visitors' room, my knees trembling. Once the receptionist at the front window pointed me to the ladies' room, I went inside to get my bearings.

Besides getting confirmation about Melinda, I also had confirmation about myself. Sure, I'd talked a good talk to Seth back there, about trusting God with his life. *"No matter what lies ahead, God will be there to guide and protect you."*

I'd parroted the words but didn't live them out. Especially with Ben. I could have said the same words to myself, that no matter what lay ahead, God would guide Ben and me and protect us. I felt like a fraud.

21

I tried not to break any speeding laws after leaving the county jail and heading back to Greenburg. Jerry would want to know what Seth told me. He should have enough proof to at least question Melinda. My pulse pounded. Until now, I hadn't been 100 percent sure Melinda had been behind the whole scenario, but I realized Seth had nothing more to lose.

My heart leaped when my Jeep rounded the corner to Ben's driveway and I saw his tractor rig. What was he doing home already? I decided to waylay Jerry before seeing Ben and parked behind him.

As I crunched across the gravel driveway to the side door, my thoughts took a different turn. What if I was making an assumption? What if Seth had concocted the whole story to get his charges reduced?

Stop it. I increased my pace and banged on the screen door. Jerry was probably kicked back watching the Braves play, if I guessed right. He didn't get many afternoons off, but if the Braves were playing, he sure tried to. Footsteps approached from the front of the house, along with the roar of a crowd from the television.

Jerry came into view through the kitchen. "Andi, what brings you here? Ben's out right now. I think he was planning to call you about coming for supper."

"I wasn't expecting him to be home—actually I

came to see you." At his quizzical expression, I continued. "I visited Seth Mitchell at the county lockup today. He called and asked me to come."

"That kid was in a lot of trouble while he was in school." Jerry shook his head. "A shame no one got through to him before he got arrested. With multiple counts of breaking and entering, he could be seeing some real jail time."

I nodded. "And that's why I'm here. He was the one who broke into my store."

"Do you know this for sure, or are you assuming?"

"Seth told me. He did it because Melinda Thacker blackmailed him."

Jerry held up one hand as if to push my words back at me. "Wait. That's a strong allegation. Why?"

As I explained, his features grew more thoughtful, his brow furrowed. I paused, hoping he'd give me a shred of hope that he believed Seth's story. I know I did.

"Interesting," was all he said at first.

"I think it's more than interesting. It explains why my store was broken into. Explains why Seth freaked and practically ran from the store a couple of weeks ago when he stopped by and Melinda showed up. And it explains how Melinda gained access to my scrub. If she had Seth break in for her, she could have access to the scrub without the dirty work of trying to break in herself." I wanted to cheer.

"All right, I'll put in a call to the DA."

"Can you question Melinda?" I detested the pleading sound in my voice. Not like I *wanted* her to be a murderer, but I wanted to be right for once.

Jerry rubbed his forehead and leaned on the door frame. "I've got to be really careful about who I question, when, how, and why. If Melinda's guilty, I wouldn't want to jeopardize any case against her by questioning without evidence. The Thackers have pull around here, and I wouldn't put it past them to start trouble. Which is why I talk to the DA, get a statement from Seth, and go from there."

"Thanks, Jerry." I attempted an appreciative smile. So he wasn't doing cartwheels over what I learned. But at least he was talking to the DA.

"Anytime, Andi." He nodded.

"I'll see ya." I turned to head down the steps.

The man needed someone to fuss over him and cook for him. I wondered if he felt on the outside looking in, seeing me and Ben together. Guys like Jerry lived their jobs, running a small-town police force, living out the adage of being overworked and underpaid. I almost regretted disturbing his ball game.

A familiar-sounding pickup truck roared into the driveway. Ben pulled up behind Jerry's vehicle. "Hey there! Have you eaten yet? I'm going to fry up some Bongo burgers."

I shook my head. "I'm famished." After the trip back and forth from the county jail, it was long past lunchtime and heading straight for supper. The day's events had caught up with me. Seth's confession, the confirmation of my suspicions, and the idea that Ben had been avoiding me clamored for attention in my head.

Ben gave me a hug on the doorstep. Had I imagined his avoidance for the past week or so? I also wondered why he was home again.

"You're home so soon."

"I got halfway to Cleveland and got called back. I have to head to Jackson first thing in the morning." Ben grinned. "C'mon in. Got some iced tea made, unless Jerry drank it all."

I followed him into the house and filled him in on what was going on with Seth, and about Melinda. "But I still feel like I need to get that evidence, at least get some answers for myself."

Ben filled a glass with tea, set it on the table, and pushed the sugar in my direction. "Let Jerry do his job." He turned to take a plate of burgers from the fridge and got a frying pan oiled up and waiting for the burgers.

My stomach growled. "What if they won't listen to Seth? It's going to be his word against hers, and right now with the position he's in, I don't think they'll take him very seriously. And then we'll be right back where we started."

"Didn't Jerry say he'd help?" Ben placed the seasoned burgers on the frying pan. The surface sizzled and popped. "Oh yeah, smell that already."

"He did say that, but matters are out of Jerry's hands."

"Then they're out of your hands, too."

I bit my lip, took a sip of tea, and decided against telling him about the food dehydrator. For now. "I see what you mean."

"Do me—do *us* a favor. Let it go for tonight."

My earlier twinges of unease started to disappear. "I missed you."

"I've been gone longer than this before." When he turned to face me, his expression remained passive.

"I know, but I couldn't reach you. Is something wrong with your phone?"

When he didn't respond at first, I started to wonder if I'd been right about him avoiding me. My unease reared up once again. What if Ben was hiding something? This reminded me of my earlier thoughts, the words I'd spoken to Seth about trusting God.

"I'm here now." He took the ketchup and mustard out of the fridge. "And I'm sorry I didn't get your calls."

"I'm glad you're here." I sipped my tea and tried not to concentrate on his last cryptic statement but instead on what I'd learned that afternoon. "I have a confession to make."

"Oh?"

"Talking to Seth today made me realize how much I still have to learn about trusting God, especially with the future. Our future." My throat constricted.

Ben settled onto the chair across from me and took my hand. "I have a lot to learn, too."

"But you're so sure of yourself."

He shook his head. "Don't you think there are times I've been out on the road and wondered if I'd come home and find you'd lost interest in me? Or times I wonder if I'm making a mistake in coming home off the road for good?"

"I hadn't thought about that." How could I be so clueless and only think about my own feelings? "Ben, I'm sorry. There's never been anyone but you. Even while you were gone. And I do support you in your decision, even though the unknown can be scary."

"Oh, Ands." He caressed my cheek. "I wasn't trying to make you feel bad. I was saying I've not always been sure about everything, either. But I believe in God's guidance. And I believe in us."

"I do, too." My stomach growled, and we both chuckled.

"When did you last eat?"

"Um, last night?" I watched him pull some plates from the shelf.

"See, that's your problem. You need to make time to eat." Ben stacked burgers on a plate. "Grab the fixings, and we can eat in the living room. I rented a movie. Jerry's crashed in the den watching the game, so we'll be out of each other's way. He'll follow the smell of the food if he's hungry."

"Ooh, a movie!" I picked up the plate of sliced tomatoes and onions and found the chips. "What'd you get?"

"Alfred Hitchcock. *Rear Window.*"

"I haven't seen that in ages." His thoughtful gesture warmed me. Usually he picked something a tad more action packed. Okay, a lot more action packed. But I love older suspense movies, and *Rear Window* is one of my favorites. This was a good sign. Ben's mysterious mood had vanished.

As nightfall approached, Ben and I settled onto his

lumpy love seat once he'd popped the DVD into the player. The more I watched, the faster the wheels in my head turned. A suspicion of murder. Jimmy Stewart's and Grace Kelly's characters trying to figure out what happened to the man's wife across the way.

What made me sit up and really take notice was how they called Lars Thorwald's bluff. Although I'd seen the movie more than a dozen times, I hadn't thought of the correlation between my situation and theirs. My pulse quickened when I saw Lisa Fremont and her boyfriend write the note to the villain that said, "What have you done with her?"

If I were to find the connection between Melinda and the food dehydrator, I'd have to find a way to draw her out, to see if she still had it.

After I refilled my iced tea glass in the kitchen, I sat next to Ben again. "You know, I've noticed a similarity between the movie and what's going on with Melinda. I'm not going to break into her apartment, but I *am* going to see if I can call her out."

"So what are you going to do? Write her a note?" Ben gestured to the television screen as Lisa ran across the courtyard to Lars Thorwald's apartment and slid the envelope under the door.

"That's *exactly* what I'm going to do." I set my glass on the coffee table. "Do you have any notepaper or a legal pad or something? And a marker."

Ben shook his head. "I was just kidding."

"Well, I'm not. Really. Paper and a pen or something."

"I happen to agree with Doyle, the detective buddy in *Rear Window*. That's a private world we're looking into."

I stood and went to the kitchen. "It is, and if nothing comes of this idea, so be it. At least I tried. Now, about that notepad? Don't you have a place where you keep your bills or paper or something?" I shouldn't have been so hard on him. For a guy, he's remarkably organized.

Ben met me in the kitchen and pulled out a drawer. "Here. Since you're so insistent." He withdrew a notepad and pen. "Want an envelope, too?"

"That would be wonderful." I sat down at the kitchen table. "I need to say something direct yet simple. Okay. How about this?" I wrote in block letters, as carefully as I could: "Melinda, I know what you did. And I know how you did it." Then I held up my handiwork. "What do you think?"

"I think you're something else." He tapped the note. "So what do you plan to do?"

"I'm going to do a stakeout. You got your binoculars handy?" If I sounded a little intense, so be it, but thanks to Jimmy Stewart and Grace Kelly, I knew I'd get to the bottom of this. I followed him back to the living room.

"A stakeout." Ben moved to open the front door and let the cool evening breeze drift through. He paused the movie. "Andi, stop. You don't have to go to all this trouble."

"Don't you have binoculars?"

"Aren't you listening to me? Drop it. Enough."

"A woman died. Someone killed her. I'm tired of this hanging over my head and waiting for this to *end*."

"Well, I feel the same way."

"What's that supposed to mean?"

"Never mind." Ben sank back onto the love seat. A roar from the den and a shout from Jerry told me *his* night was going well.

"I could be wrong."

"And if you're not. . ."

"Poor Melinda. . ." My stomach caught. What if Melinda had only intended to scare her sister, maybe mess up her wedding photos—not kill her? Of course, I didn't know how long Melinda had known she was pregnant. "But if she did this without trying to kill Charla. . .maybe it won't go too badly for Melinda." My head hurt.

"You could just talk to her, tell her what you know." Ben squeezed my hand.

"Give her a chance to explain." I sighed. "Especially now that she's lost the baby."

"You're so compassionate, and I love that about you." He put his arm around me. "Take your time and choose your words carefully."

"I will." I forced my attention back to the television. At last, "THE END" flashed across the screen. I tried not to yawn, but Ben beat me to it.

"Guess I'll go," I said as I stood and stretched. "I know you're tired."

He nodded and gave me a sleepy smile. "But I enjoyed the evening."

"Can. . .can I borrow your binoculars, just in case?"

Ben groaned and stood, then went to his gun cabinet and pulled some binoculars out of a bottom drawer. "Stubborn woman."

"You are such a sweetheart." I accepted the binoculars and hugged him. "I might not even need them."

"You're going to do this tonight?"

I nodded. "I can't afford to wait." I slung the binoculars strap over my shoulder and reached for my purse, tucking the letter neatly inside.

Ben gave me a quick hug and a kiss. "I'll see you when I get back."

"I'll be waiting to hear from you." I wanted to add, "Don't forget to call me while you're on the road," but I didn't. He would be home again soon enough, with everything the future would bring us.

It wasn't too much after nine, and I hoped Melinda would be home for the evening, as well. Someone on a stakeout never knew how long they'd have to wait. I figured I ought to bring a variety of snacks and drinks to keep me alert. My Jeep needed gas, so I dropped by a convenience store on the way into town and filled up. After my debit card recovered from the shock, I bought three sodas and some yogurt-covered pretzels.

I found my way down the darkened streets of Greenburg and turned onto the street where Emily and Melinda lived. My heart thudded. What on earth was I doing? I'd blazed a trail from Ben's place all the way here, and I was sure if I looked over my shoulder, I'd probably see flames trailing behind me.

After I parked the Jeep behind a pickup near the corner, I peered through the binoculars. I could see the glow of the porch light in front of Melinda and Emily's home. Both women's cars were in the driveway. Minutes ticked by. For a while I listened to the radio and tried to hold off eating my snacks. After all, I'd had a great Bongo burger at Ben's. If someone had told me that morning I'd end up staking out Melinda Thacker's house, I probably wouldn't have believed them.

I remembered my earlier train of thought. Did I care about Melinda, or was I just trying to prove my point? Maybe Ben was right. Instead of trying to slip her the letter anonymously, I would try a direct approach. Maybe then Melinda would talk to me, say something, and then we could go and talk to Jerry together. I knew I couldn't sleep tonight otherwise.

Putting the Jeep into first gear, I headed the rest of the way to Melinda's house and parked in front of her driveway. *Lord, help. I can't do like they did to Lars Thorwald.* I just wanted to talk to her. I knew she trusted me. I just couldn't sneak. Well, not until I gave her a chance to talk.

So I pounded on the door.

The screen door swung open. Melinda's fair skin looked almost pasty in the porch light. "Oh, um, hi. What brings you here?"

"I. . .I wanted to talk to you about something. I

couldn't over the phone." Just then I realized I hadn't planned on what to say. "Er, how are you feeling?"

"Better every day." Her slight smile provided a scant mask for the pain I saw reflected in her eyes.

"Good." I rubbed my arms. A hot, sticky Tennessee night, and I had goose bumps. "I need to talk about the day Charla died. I know that's painful for you, but I've learned some things that you should know."

She licked her lips and blinked. "Another conspiracy theory?"

"No. Someone broke into my store. That's how the facial scrub got sabotaged. But I don't think someone was *trying* to kill Charla. I don't think they meant it. Maybe they were trying to scare her, or teach her a lesson, or ruin her wedding." I made myself stop. A cricket chirped somewhere in the night. In other circumstances, this would have been funny. Somewhere out toward Main Street someone honked a car horn.

"Is that what you think?"

"I do. Does that idea sound possible?"

"I don't know." Melinda shook her head.

"It was dried strawberries. I found the seeds in the scrub. This points to several people. You said that Emily even admitted to giving Charla strawberry candy or something last summer as revenge. And then what about Mike Chandler? Charla sued him for trying to 'poison' her. Or worse, what if Robert was trying to get out of the wedding for some reason? A little extreme, but if he was seeing someone else. . ." I'd already blown the theory about Robert, but I needed to see what Melinda would say.

"I—said—I—don't—know!" She brushed away a tear. "Just go. Please go."

"Melinda, do you know something?" *Please. . .*my throat hurt. "If it was an accident—"

"Go—" The wooden door slammed shut behind the screen. Off went the porch light.

I trudged to my Jeep and launched into prayer. "I tried, I did. Lord, I never thought it would be this hard." My own eyes burned as I drove away from Melinda's house. At the end of the street, I waited. A niggle in my stomach told me I ought to go back to where I'd hung out and debated with myself not long ago. So I circled the block and tucked the Jeep behind the pickup again and waited.

22

Three hours later, I'd cleared through my bagful of yogurt-covered pretzels and all three sodas. I squinted through the binoculars at the front porch of Melinda and Emily's place.

C'mon, Melinda. I staved off the late-night mental fog and glanced at my watch. Midnight had come and gone. Maybe I should have brought something with a little more caffeine in it.

And maybe I'd been wrong. There was that possibility. Maybe Seth was a good liar. Maybe I'd made assumptions about that private world I was looking into, thinking back to the line from *Rear Window.*

My pulse rate jumped at least twenty beats when I saw a rectangle of light in front of the darkened house. Someone was coming out, leaving the porch light off. And that someone held a box and a lumpy garbage bag. Donation time!

Melinda carried the items to her car. The streetlight gave me a good view. When she glanced up and down the street, I shrank down a bit. Then I realized I should have brought Di's sensible minivan, a carbon copy of so many others in Greenburg. I flopped sideways across the passenger seat, praying all the while that Melinda did not see me. As a sleuth, I had definitely not thought of everything. Besides that, the sodas had kicked in and I *really* needed a bathroom.

The lights from Melinda's car reflected off the interior of the Jeep as she passed. Only when the street darkened again did I dare sit up. I threw the Jeep into gear and whirled it around, then slipped out onto the main street. Did she take a left or a right? I saw a pair of red taillights attached to a dark hard-top convertible ahead. There she was. I followed but not too closely.

My phone warbled. I tapped the speaker button. "Di?"

"Andromeda Clark, where are you?"

"Now's not really a good time to talk," I said above the rumble of the engine.

"I called the house, and when you didn't answer, I was worried."

"I'm following Melinda Thacker."

"What?"

"I can't explain right now, but I think she's trying to get rid of her food dehydrator." Melinda hung a right, as if she were headed to Value-Mart.

"Oh, I wish I could have helped out, but Stevie's been sick tonight. Poor baby. I wish this stomach bug would leave our house once and for all."

"Don't worry about it. He needs you." I hollered the words as I downshifted.

"I'll let you go. Be careful."

"I will. And give Stevie a hug for me." I ended the call then downshifted again as I approached Value-Mart's parking lot. Nothing open except a gas station back down the street and Value-Mart with a cluster of cars in front. What a scandal when the store stayed open twenty-four hours after the big corporate remodel.

Melinda headed across the parking lot to the strip mall next to Value-Mart. It dawned on me that she probably had a clear view of my Jeep, so I turned into the drive-through lane of Burger Barn (also open twenty-four hours). When I was in high school, it was the only place you could get a burger after midnight. Still is.

The worker at the order window slid back the glass door when I drove up.

"Sorry, I'm not placing an order." I waved at the cashier and circled around behind the restaurant. I kept an eye on Melinda's car, the parking lot lights glinting off the blue metal. Now she was heading past the corner of the building.

I assumed the strand of stores had a garbage receptacle in the back. Melinda was a smart cookie, getting rid of the evidence somewhere besides her place. I paused in the restaurant parking lot and waited until I saw Melinda's car emerge from the shadowed end of the line of stores. She drove back the way she came, intent on her journey.

Then I drove the same route that Melinda had taken. When I rounded the corner of the minimall, the rear entries of the storefronts were lit by a solitary streetlamp. The sight of half a dozen trash bins greeted me.

Some sleuth I was. I hadn't counted on each store having its own bin. Worse, I didn't even have a flashlight with me. Was this a fool's errand, a quirky coincidence? Maybe I should have stayed at Ben's a little longer and talked about our future and let this crazy idea go. I shouldn't have left him, especially considering how strange he'd been acting lately. Momma always said avoiding a problem was worse than meeting it head-on. If you met it head-on, it couldn't sneak around behind you. When Ben returned home again, I wouldn't run off. But I couldn't deny that my questions for Melinda tonight had definitely struck a nerve and spurred her into action.

I sighed as I pointed the front of the Jeep at the first trash bin and slid the gearshift to PARK, taking care to pull the emergency brake. When I slid from the driver's seat of the Jeep, the nighttime breeze wafted the odor of garbage in my direction. No matter how bad it smelled, I would see this thing through to the end. Di and Ben ought to be proud of my determination not to quit when the going got smelly.

A sign above the back of the first store told me I was at the rear entrance for China Café. *Oh, please, not in this bin.* The edge of the rusted steel contraption stood just slightly above my eye level. I hopped, trying to catch a glimpse of the contents. Just black plastic bags and flattened cardboard boxes, partly covered in shadow.

I jumped back into the Jeep. On to the next one. I shook my head. Melinda couldn't have been long in tossing away the dehydrator box and the garbage bag. I squinted to see the signs for the rest of the stores.

Salvation Army. What better place to donate used items, especially ones that were good sellers? I drove the Jeep down to that trash bin. A flash of headlights from a passing car on the street made me look up. No, Melinda wasn't going to return. She would go home, get into her jammies, and try her best to sleep.

The bright red bin beckoned me as if it contained a treasure. If only it weren't so tall. Maybe I could vault onto the edge and balance at the top to see down inside it, then grab the food dehydrator box and make sure I had the right one.

My plan was simple. If I found the food dehydrator, I would take it. No, not steal it. I would write a note to Jennifer Toms, who ran the store, and leave a donation in their mail slot at the front of the mini-mall.

Bracing my hands on the edge of the bin, I vaulted onto the edge as planned. There it was! The Dry-It-Fast food dehydrator, normally sold at Value-Mart for forty dollars, once owned by Melinda Thacker. If I was careful, I'd have the long-sought-for evidence. That "means" Jerry needed. On its own, the food dehydrator didn't matter. But pile it together with the other evidence. . .

My forward momentum didn't stop, and I crashed onto a lumpy trash bag. Clothing oozed from the split bag. I reached for the food dehydrator box as if it were the holy grail.

Now, how to get out of here? I let the box balance on the flat corner of the trash bin then reached for the edge once again and slung my legs over the side.

But wait. This was evidence. I could tell Jerry it was here and that I was 90 sure Melinda had dropped it here, that I'd followed her to this alley. He could send people here or whatever he needed to do so someone could legally pick it up. I dropped to my feet and took the box down from the corner of the trash bin.

A pair of headlights approached, and I squinted at the vehicle. Greenburg is not a town where one should be afraid after dark. But tonight, past midnight, in the shadowy backside of a mini-mall, I trembled.

Then a police siren chirped and a set of blue and red strobes lit up the night. "Freeze—Greenburg PD!"

23

"M a'am, put the box down, and put your hands on your head." The officer crossed the short distance between his car and the trash bin.

I closed my eyes and obeyed. "This is a mistake, really; I'm not trying to rob. . ." Every arrest scene from every cop show I'd ever seen flashed through my mind.

"You are under arrest. You have the right to remain silent—"

"Listen, Officer, Jerry Hartley's practically my brother-in-law." If any doubts remained in my mind about Ben and our future, they'd been replaced by the scenes from cop shows. I just *couldn't* be arrested.

"—can and will be held against you in a court of law."

Various protests teetered on the tip of my tongue. *Shut—up—shut—up—shut—up.* I kept my mouth closed.

My arms were drawn downward. No one ever told me how much that hurt, but then I'd never been arrested, either. Cold steel handcuffs circled my wrists. I bit my lip. All I'd wanted was the stupid food dehydrator. Sort of. But if I tried telling the officer I was just putting it back, I suspected I wouldn't convince him.

"Let's go." Officer Go-Get-'Em took me by the elbow and escorted me to the waiting car, its lights flashing. "That store's been complaining of thieves making off with donations in the evenings, and they'll be glad to know I got someone."

But you've got the wrong someone! I slid onto the rear seat of the squad car, behind the metal mesh that divided the front from the back. When the door slammed, I clamped my eyes shut. Blue and red strobes pulsated through my eyelids.

I opened my eyes to watch the officer radio for a tow truck for my Jeep. He had the swagger of a young twentysomething when he headed back to the trash bin. Of course he slipped on some latex gloves. Then with a flourish and half grin, he toted the food dehydrator box to the back of the squad car and stuffed it into the trunk.

We waited until the tow truck came to take my Jeep to the impound. Then the fine young rookie climbed behind the wheel of his car, radioed that he was taking a female perpetrator to the station, and we were off. I wiggled on the seat so I could glimpse the triumphant grin on his face.

"Please, Officer. You don't know. . ."

When he shot me a backward glance, I closed my mouth again. I did have one phone call. That much I knew. I'd probably have to sit in the town jail at least overnight. Would bail have to be posted?

What would Ben say? No way would I call him tonight and hear "I told you so." I refused to cry as the squad car moved through the deserted streets of Greenburg. One final trip as a trucker, and Ben would come back to *this* news. In the paper. Whispered in restaurants. Scandal like this was good fodder for at least a couple months' gossip. And thereafter, whenever anyone talked about garbage receptacles or Salvation Army or Andi Clark's crazy stunts.

First Charla's death at my store, and now this. Jerry would have to straighten everything out for me. But I wouldn't call him until I knew Ben had left for Jackson. Pride, I know. Even for me this was way over the top.

Once I'd been fingerprinted and photographed, I stood at the phone and trembled. I didn't want to bother my parents. Momma and Daddy didn't need my news. Not tonight, anyway.

Di answered on the second ring, her voice tentative and strained. She was probably puzzled by the "Greenburg PD" that I imagine popped up on her caller ID. Especially after it woke her from a sound sleep, unless she was still cleaning up after a sick kid.

"Di, I'm in jail, and I need your help."

"Jail!" Di's shriek made me jerk the phone from my ear.

"Don't say anything to Momma and Daddy." I lowered my voice as I told her about the food dehydrator. "Fortunately, the overeager rookie brought it back here as the alleged evidence. My fingerprints are on that box, but so are Melinda Thacker's."

"But what about you?"

"I'm okay. Can you come and get me?"

Fleta the bailiff laughed from across the booking room. "You can ask someone to come down tonight all you want. But they can't post bail until morning."

I tried not to frown at Fleta. It wasn't my fault I didn't know the bail procedure. And where was sweet Anna who ran the desk out front during the day? Home asleep, like the other law-abiding citizens.

"I could try to get away," Di said. "Stevie's throwing up now, and Steve's not much better. . . . Can you give me awhile?"

"Never mind. Get some rest tonight. I just learned I have to wait until *tomorrow* to get bailed out."

"I'll try to come in the morning or see if Daddy can. Someone will come for you."

After that, we ended our call. Fleta gave a chuckle when I hung up the phone. She tapped my elbow and escorted me back to one of the three cells in the jailhouse. "In you go."

"Fleta. . .please. . .this is all a misunderstanding." As if my trying to play the "I'm practically family" card had worked before.

"I can't do you any favors, and you know that." The cell door clanged as she slid it closed. "What if word got around?"

A small cot jutted out from one wall. I sank onto its lumpy mattress. "I know, I know."

She flashed a toothy grin at me. "Then it'll keep 'til tomorrow, and we'll get it all figured it out then." The radio squawked from the front office, and its sound echoed to the back where the cells were located—where I currently sat, trying not to glare at Fleta's retreating form.

I rolled onto my back and looked at the fluorescent light, which had just commenced blinking. Maybe if I asked, Fleta would turn it off. Or maybe there were rules against turning out lights in cell blocks. Someone down the hall snored.

Common sense told me I should cry or spend the night worrying, but at that moment, I realized the truth of what I'd mentioned to Di earlier. The food dehydrator was safely in custody, too. If I'd tried to drag that down to the station myself, it probably wouldn't count as evidence. But brought in carefully and tagged by the good young officer. . .

"Lord, I've messed up plenty tonight," I whispered. Hopefully the snorer wouldn't be disturbed by my prayers. "But I know You're with me, and I'm okay. I'll probably never live this down. But it doesn't matter." I rolled onto my side. The mattress smelled only slightly stale, and I wondered if someone doused it with fabric deodorizer regularly.

I tried not to give in to the feeling of a caged leopard. No wonder they wanted to pace. I'd just lost the last of my personal control, and I fought off the sensation of the walls and bars closing in. I'd fought so hard against being controlled by people's expectations—the town, my parents, Di, Ben, add any other name I could think of. And some of those people (I wasn't totally convinced about the town) loved me. They were only trying to help. Which made me fight harder.

"I'm sorry, Lord. I surrender to You. You've given me so much: my family, Ben, my business. Friends.

You have more for me, too, and I've been letting fear and stubbornness hold me back. I can't do this alone, pushing people away and trying to figure everything out. I can't." I brushed away a tear.

In spite of my disastrous sleuthing, God had a reason for me being right in this little cell. Talk about getting corralled long enough to get some sense drilled into me. God had been loving me through my family, Di, and Ben, and I'd missed it.

I prayed for I don't know how long, a running conversation about anything and everything. Though I found myself stuck behind metal bars, I felt free. I couldn't stop the smile. Ironic, me fighting that old trapped feeling, and now it had disappeared in jail. I could hardly wait to reach Ben and pick out some house plans.

———

"Baby girl, what have you gone and done?" The door to the cellblock clanged behind Daddy as he burst through it the following morning. He still wore his house slippers, which said a lot for Daddy, who never went anywhere without his work boots.

"It's a long story." I met him at the cell bars. "I'll pay you back."

He waved me off and shook his head. "I talked to Jerry, and they'll get you to see the judge as soon as they can. He said the charges will likely get thrown out."

"Daddy, I need to get him to check that food

dehydrator from the Salvation Army trash bin. It's got fingerprints on it."

"Don't tell me it's true, then?" A look of shock crossed his face. "You really tried to steal from them? We raised you right, girl!"

"No, it's not that. I was standing there with the box, and I'd realized I ought to put it back instead of leaving a note and a donation in the store drop box, when the officer drove up and arrested me." I clutched the bars and sucked in a breath. "He wouldn't listen and started reading me my rights."

"Well, let's get going." Daddy glanced over his shoulder. "Jerry, open this door right now."

"Yessir, Mr. Clark." Jerry fumbled with the keys, and I tried not to glare at him. "Andi, I'm sorry about what happened." Jerry leaned closer when I passed through the cell door. "I know this case will get tossed out. My overeager rookie's going to need a refresher course."

I bit my tongue. "Jerry, you've got to check the prints on that dehydrator. Not just the box."

Daddy held up a bag I hadn't noticed before. "Got us some breakfast bagel-wiches from Honey's. Ham, egg, and cheese for me. Bacon, egg, and cheese for you. Coffee in the truck."

My stomach growled. "Oh." My throat swelled, and I was eight again, with Daddy making everything right.

We climbed into his ancient pickup, reserved for runs to the town dump and trips to the recycling plant, and now probably designated for picking up jailbird daughters after posting bail. My eyelids drooped once I fastened the seat belt.

Then I opened them. "Could you please run me by my store real quick? I need to pick something up and bring it back to Jerry." I smiled at Daddy and took a bite of my bagel-wich.

<hr>

Jerry looked surprised when Daddy dropped me by the station forty minutes later. I lugged in the large cherry scrub container from the party. "Andi. Back again. You forgot your purse. Fleta's got it."

"Thanks." I put the scrub on the counter. "Brought you something."

"Come to my office. We'll chat." He motioned, and I followed him behind the glass partition. He closed the door behind us.

I took a deep breath before starting. "This is the container of scrub from Charla's party. Did you check the bowl of scrub for fingerprints—Charla's bowl that you took the day she died?"

"Well, no, can't say as I have. Didn't see the need at the time. Just sent the soap for testing." He looked thoughtful, but he wasn't stopping me, and I took that as a good sign.

"Okay then. I'm asking you again to test everything. The food dehydrator, the container, and Charla's bowl. I believe all three will have the same fingerprints."

"And you think those will belong to. . . ?"

"Melinda Thacker." I spoke her name aloud and felt a sinking sensation in the pit of my stomach. "If I'm wrong, so be it. But I think you need to check."

Jerry settled onto his office chair and steepled his fingers underneath his chin. "I seem to remember Melinda got picked up for shoplifting back in high school. We'd have her prints on file."

I nodded as I played my final card. "I know it's a long shot. But I've had a suspicion about the strawberries ever since the beginning. After this, if nothing comes up, I'll drop the idea. But if this helps you when you talk to the DA about Seth. . ."

He said nothing for a moment, so I pounced again.

"You owe me this much. I did the hard work for y'all and got arrested in the process. But I know this was Melinda's, because I followed her to the store last night when she dumped it off. Literally."

"Andi, I gotta tell you, it sounds like a long shot. We'll see what we find. And if we have a match, I'll bring her in."

"Thanks, Jerry."

As I left the station after getting my purse back from Fleta, my heart sank. I shouldn't feel triumphant about this. Not if it ruined a woman's life.

I worked at the store for two days after meeting with Jerry. The time crawled. I tried calling Ben but couldn't get through. A sleepless night greeted me every night I trudged to bed. I had so much to tell him. Then I tagged along with Di and the boys to the city park pool in the afternoon. The whole time Di and I lounged poolside while the boys splashed around, all I could see was the winding road that passed the pool, entered the woods, and ended at the lodge where I'd seen Emily pleading with Robert.

And so my thoughts circled back to Melinda. My heart broke for her. My gut told me, though, that her revenge had cooked a long, slow burn. This wasn't an "Oops, sorry about the strawberries getting into your scrub" mistake. This was an "I'm going to enjoy making you pay" kind of payback. Besides, she'd gotten Seth to break into the store, I reminded myself.

"Hey, wake up." Di touched my arm. "Your tote bag is ringing."

I jerked upright in the lounge chair, knocked my towel into a puddle of water, and fumbled for the phone. *Jerry.* "Do you have news?"

"We do. Melinda's prints are all over everything. Her prints are on Charla's bowl and inside the large vat of that cherry scrub. Yours are all over everything, too, by the way. Except for the food dehydrator."

"That's not funny. Besides, I have no motive."

"True." I heard his chair creak. "Officer Chubb is on his way to pick up Melinda now. I had that chat with the DA about Seth and shared your theories with him. He said to bring her in."

"Just like that?"

"Just like that."

I suppose I shouldn't have been surprised when my phone rang ten minutes later. And it was Melinda.

"What did you tell them?"

"Melinda, I tried to talk to you. . ." A child in the pool shrieked, and I clamped the phone more tightly to my ear.

"So that's what you were trying to do the other night? Talk to me? And now the cops are picking me up to come to the station for questioning. You know, you could have left well enough alone. My parents are going to freak. Between you and my stupid cousin. . ." Melinda's voice shook. "Did you know my daddy's planning to run for a state representative position? I guess not now."

"I only wanted the truth."

"Oh, no, there's a squad car pulling up out front—" The line went dead.

Di was hollering at one of the boys to get off the diving board. Once they obeyed, she turned back to me. "What's goin' on?"

"Melinda Thacker's getting brought in for questioning."

"Boys—we're leavin'!" Di leaped to her feet.

Clad in my damp shorts and shirt, I waved 'bye to Diana. My still-damp flip-flops squeaked as I climbed the steps of the police station. *Melinda.* In spite of what she'd done, my heart went out to her. Maybe I'd get turned away, but I wanted to talk to her face-to-face.

I found Melinda in the main reception area. Her shoulders were slumped, and whoever had brought her in was filling out some paperwork at the desk.

Melinda looked up. "I can't believe you had the nerve to show up here. Daddy said I ought to call a lawyer before I talk to them. So I did. And I'm coming straight after you once this mess is over with."

I sat next to her on the bench. "I. . .I know about the baby, Melinda." I reached to touch her shoulder. Where was Jerry? I caught a glimpse of him through the glass window of his office. He was on the phone, nodding and glancing my way.

A wail rose from Melinda, and she wrapped her arms around her chest, drawing away from me. "I loved it. I wanted it. Him, her. It didn't matter. And Robert never knew." She hunched over in the chair. "He wouldn't even talk to me. Emily tried to get him to listen, but he moved on. Then on the Fourth, I saw him with the backstabbing little—"

My throat tied itself in a knot. "You had Seth break into my store. No one believed him. At first."

Melinda straightened her posture. A wave of desperation and rage broke across me when she glanced my way. "Blood is thicker than water, they say. I saw Seth and his little goonies breaking into a store one night in May. Told him I'd turn him in if he didn't help me get into that ridiculous shop of yours."

This wasn't exactly a confession or new information. And my store *wasn't* ridiculous, but I reminded myself this was a Thacker talking. I bit my lip.

I saw Jerry quietly enter the reception area through a door behind Melinda.

"I have nothing left to lose. Not since Robert refused to acknowledge our love, not since Charla continues to ruin my life even though she's rotting in the grave."

At that, I flinched.

"Mike Chandler has the best strawberries in the county, did you know? Sweet revenge, no pun intended."

"So, enter the food dehydrator," I said aloud.

"You're smart. I knew that. I should have figured you'd know something was wrong with the cherry scrub." She flipped her walnut-colored hair over one shoulder, her almond eyes round and reddened. "But I enjoyed drying those berries. Every moment, I thought of Charla's face when she realized what she'd done to herself. With her own hands. And all I had to do was watch."

"So you meant to kill her?" My chest hurt.

Melinda clamped her mouth shut, then continued. "I didn't say that. I was sick and tired of it all. With me and Robert, it was flames from the beginning, especially when Charla wouldn't give him what he wanted." Melinda smiled at me, still oblivious to Jerry standing behind her. "Oh yeah, I see your shock. Charla wasn't the town high-class floozy that some thought. She had standards, and when a guy got too close, she took off running. Funny how rumors get started, don't you think? By the time Charla keeled over, she had enough enemies. She also had plenty of strawberry in her system, here and there, that I fed her."

"So the cumulative effect of the allergen in her system pushed her body over the edge once she used that scrub." I shook my head.

All I saw was a broken soul that had given up the struggle.

"Don't look at me like that, Andi Clark." Melinda's eyes flashed with renewed fire. "You should have quit nosing around. Your business would have bounced back. You know how it is around here. Someone else would have been the big news in Greenburg eventually."

"That's true enough," I admitted. "But some questions had to be answered."

"Why didn't you just mind your own business? And don't give me that 'I-know-what-it's-like-to-be-disappointed-in-love' speech. You've got someone that any woman in her right mind would fight to keep. I thought I did. . . ."

My gaze flicked to Jerry as I rose, then shot back down at Melinda. There didn't seem a reason for me to be here. "I'm praying for you, Melinda, and I did want to be your friend."

"Save your breath." She stared at the floor.

Jerry said, "Ms. Thacker, would you like to give a statement now?"

The station was a blur as I passed through it and headed to the main doors. My throat hurt, and I dashed tears away. I didn't know how I could deal with the idea that I was actually right about Melinda. I'd wanted answers and made assumptions but hadn't paused long enough to consider the ramifications of the answers.

Once I hit the bright outdoors, I let the tears come. I slammed into someone. Hard. I squinted up into the glare of the sun. "Ben!"

He had his arms around me in an instant and let me sob as he rubbed my back. "I'm home, baby, for good," I heard him whisper. "What's wrong?"

"It was Melinda. I thought I'd be happy if I knew the truth, but I'm not. She's being questioned inside right now."

"Honey, you tried." His hug felt good. "I wasn't happy the other night when you didn't listen to me, but I know why you were so determined."

"You. . .you're home early." I smiled at him.

"Di called me that night. Said you were in trouble. I came back as soon as I could." He released me only enough so we could look each other in the eyes. "I wasn't avoiding you the last time I was home, but I had some important business to tend to. It was either keep my phone off or risk ruining my surprise. When you get it in your head to find something out, there's no stopping you."

"I'm really glad you're here." My nose was running, so I fumbled for a tissue in my purse.

"Here's what kept me away. Had to find it, order it. Then it was on back order so I had to go somewhere else to pick it up 'cause I didn't want to wait."

Numb, I nodded, still looking for a tissue. By the time I found one and blew my nose, Ben had produced a small velvet box and gotten down on one knee. I dropped my purse and grabbed my throat.

"Andromeda Clark," Ben said in a husky voice, "I have loved you for too long without making the commitment to you that I should have. I want to be with you always. I want your face to be the first thing I see in the morning—"

"Oh, you poor thing, I get real bad bedhead."

"Stop. I'm tryin' to do this right so we can tell our children all about it someday."

Children. Oh. I'd think about that another time. But what a ring. The diamond flashed with the glimmer of a star that had been plucked from the sky and inserted in a gold setting.

"I'm sorry. Go ahead. I need to learn to be quiet." My hands trembled. In truth, I'd dreamed of a day like this. I wanted to be with him always, to learn to live with him as his wife. Maybe we were older than the average couple, but we still had plenty of years to build a wonderful life together.

Ben cleared his throat. "I want your face to be the first thing I see in the morning and the last thing I see at night. I'm tired of being on the road, and I want to live the adventure at home. With you. Say you'll marry me, Ands."

"Oh, I will!"

With that, he slid the diamond solitaire onto my finger, and we sealed the agreement with a kiss. *"Adventure,"* he said? Did he mean adventure by planning a wedding, building a house, running a business, and getting used to being around each other all the time? *Well, bring it on.*

Lynette Sowell has written four novellas and a Heartsong Presents romance novel for Barbour. This is her first published mystery. She believes stories should take readers on an entertaining ride and offer glimpses of God's truth along the way. Lynette lives in Central Texas with her husband, two teenagers, and five cats. You can learn more about Lynette and her writing at www.lynettesowell.com.

You may correspond with this author by writing:
Lynette Sowell
Author Relations
PO Box 721
Uhrichsville, OH 44683

A Letter to Our Readers

Dear Reader:
In order to help us satisfy your quest for more great mystery stories, we would appreciate it if you would take a few minutes to respond to the following questions. We welcome your comments and read each form and letter we receive. When completed, please return to:

Fiction Editor
Heartsong Presents—MYSTERIES!
PO Box 721
Uhrichsville, Ohio 44683

Did you enjoy reading *A Suspicion of Strawberries* by Lynette Sowell?

Very much! I would like to see more books like this! The one thing I particularly enjoyed about this story was:

_____

_____

_____

Moderately. I would have enjoyed it more if:

_____

_____

_____

Are you a member of the HP—MYSTERIES! Book Club?
Yes   No

If no, where did you purchase this book?

_____

Please rate the following elements using a scale of 1 (poor) to 10 (superior):

___ Main character/sleuth   ___ Romance elements

___ Inspirational theme   ___ Secondary characters

___ Setting   ___ Mystery plot

How would you rate the cover design on a scale of 1 (poor) to 5 (superior)? _____

What themes/settings would you like to see in future **Heartsong Presents—MYSTERIES!** selections? _____
_____
_____
_____

Please check your age range:
- ◯ Under 18   ◯ 18–24
- ◯ 25–34   ◯ 35–45
- ◯ 46–55   ◯ Over 55

Name: _____

Occupation: _____

Address: _____

E-mail address: _____